Edward Williams Johns

The Silver Wedding

A romaunt du moyen âge

Edward Williams Johns

The Silver Wedding
A romaunt du moyen âge

ISBN/EAN: 9783337719814

Printed in Europe, USA, Canada, Australia, Japan

Cover: Foto ©Andreas Hilbeck / pixelio.de

More available books at **www.hansebooks.com**

HE SILVER WEDDING.

To the Author of "THE SILVER WEDDING."

————o————

Poet! in musing o'er thy lyric page,
Our thoughts are wafted to the silver age;
And prayers are breathed, that heavenward years unroll'd,
May bear thee to the age of everlasting gold.

C. LINCOLN.

RISEHOLME, LINCOLN,
    22nd December, 1875.

THE subject matter of this work sought, and required for expression, a metrical version.

With regard to the versification, it will be found to possess some peculiarities; it is based, in the main, on English pentameter for the body of the work; but for "The Legend," on the multisyllabic measure of "Christabel," modified to suit an ancient legend applied to "modern instances." In other words, the subject-matter sought to develop itself as a *sonata in speech* as it were—to record rhythmical thought expressing itself in simple rhythmical speech—under a very present influence of hearing, mentally, one of Beethoven's Sonatas.

Furthermore, although in THE SILVER WEDDING,

iambic pentameter is mainly employed, there was no hesitation in using, as the feeling might dictate, dactyles for enlivening the movement of the verse, trochees for quickening it, as well as to throw the accentuation on another part of the line, and anapæsts for _recoil._

This was preferred, as being most agreeable to the author's own ear; although in one sense, and other things being equal, it is easier to write in the formulated cadenced construction of couplet, triplet, or quartrain, than in the versification here in this work used, by as much as right-line drawing is easier than the art that guides the hand truthfully, solely through thought and feeling.

The English language, differing so thoroughly as it does from the Greek, has this in common with the Greek—the subtlety of its rhythmical expression through _accent._ Nay, more; the rhythmical power of the English tongue rests almost solely upon accent, and little, or none at all, upon the arithmetic of syllables posted up, as it were, into journals and ledgers of properly recorded feet, and properly done into a correct balance-sheet. The nation of shop-keepers and their offshoots are sufficiently careful of such method, in certain books devoted to the literature of profit and loss; but their poësy abhors it, and ever looks back to the refuge of Druid-woods and to the oak-born misletoe. And well may German critics wonder that certain writers and certain canons of criticism should seek to shackle so grievously the rhythmical flexibility (its greatest charm) of the English language,—an attempt nearly about as successful as would be an endeavour to amend the grand regular irregularity of a Gothic cathedral by drawing over its plan the lines of a Greek temple. Both styles are thoughts of God refracted through the human mind. But God thinks without confusion. So the inexorable law of hybridity, by which the Creator has bounded all forms of growth beyond certain limits, includes necessarily the form-growth of the speech of the peoples and their expression of thought; and environment of circumstance, powerful as may be its action upon these, is ever re-acted upon by the inner life-principle until development is brought back, and held true to the original type, within its never-ceasing strain.

And ever has the English tongue sought to free itself from bondage, which each successive conquest strove to impose upon its resulting composite structure. Not all the empire of Rome over Britain, or of Rome's derivative power through the French and Norman-French, or the influence of other foreign admixture, have permanently availed to alter the syntactical arrangement of the language, composite as it is, beyond the scope of its own natural laws of development, or to permanently cramp its inherent life-principle—*the rhythm of accents.*

Not unjustifiably, therefore, does this work cast off the torque—and with it, all deference to the tyranny—which a taste false to the genius of the language, and false canons of criticism have cramped around the throat of English utterance. Not unjustifiably does it claim a righteous liberty; liberty, not license; the laws of its construction are severe and exacting, and proved to be as much so now, after a year and more have elapsed since the writing

of the work, as they were felt to be during its progress.
But these laws are the *natural* exponents of that
inherent life-principle of the language, the expression
of rhythmical thought through rhythmical accent.
Thus, then, the principle of the versification of this
work is the rhythm of accents, and not of arithmetical
syllables and feet, leaving these to take heed to their
own going. And so strong was the impression of
this rhythmical accentuation upon the writer, that
he hopes he may be pardoned for mentioning that,
for weeks after the work had been completed, there
was felt a curious effect entirely analogous to that
experienced by one who, lately landed from a sea
voyage, still feels for days after, the rhythmical
movement of the vessel.

Finally, as to the versification, it may be remarked
that, for much the same reasons given above,
rhyme has been employed, dropped, or resumed
at will.

The Legend, which carries the symbolism running
through "The Dwarf," "The Boar's Head and Knife,"
"The Magic Mantle," and "The Gifts," is entirely a

growth of the work, and was suggested by a few paragraphs in Mrs. Matthew Hall's "Queens before the Conquest." The author could wish his own work might meet with sufficient favour to prompt a reference to a most interesting work of a most accomplished lady writer. Some cavil might arise as to the historical accuracy of the Legend which ascribes to King Arthur the ordainment of the Silver Wedding. To this it may be justly replied, that before the Legend can be disproved on this point, it may be necessary to prove that Arthur existed at all.

It only remains to refer to the philosophy and religious ideas of the work; and on these points it is sufficient to say, that the key to them, should any be needed, may be found in the following excerpt from that noble Hymn (the third) of Synesius, which Coleridge quotes in his *Biographia Literaria* in the original, untranslated. For a better understanding of the subject of the extract as the key referred to, the author begs leave to give here the original Greek with a translation made as literal as condensation of the thought with the rhythm would permit;—

Μύσας δὲ Νόος	"Inwardly brooding
Τὰ τὲ καὶ τὰλέγει,	Soul to itself speaketh,
Βύθον ἄρρητον	Round depth unutterable
Ἀμφιχορέυων.	Quiring about:—
Σὺ τὸ τίκτον ἔφυς,	Thou, the Begetting art,
Σὺ τὸ τικτόμενον·	Thou, the Begotten art:
Σὺ τὸ φώτιζον	Thou, the Divine Flame,
Σὺ τὸ λαμπόμενον	Thou, the outblazing Light!
Σὺ τὸ φαινόμενον	Thou, the Made-Manifest,
Σὺ τὸ κρυπτόμενον	Thou, the Hidden, deep in
Ἰδίαις ἀυγαις.	Splendours peculiar.
Ἐν καὶ πάντα	One, yet All-Things,
Ἐν καθ' ἑαυτὸ	One, as Itself lone,
Καὶ διὰ πάντων	Yet throughout All-Things."

Lo, here, a magnificent symbol of The Incarnation! and in a secondary sense, the Soul, Mind, or Νόος, shut in upon itself (μύω, or μύζω) may be supposed as addressing itself, through its union with God, as a duality, with the higher Christian Pantheism of

St. Paul—that is, as itself in God, of God, or as part of God, who is All, in All, and above All.

To Him, the All-Father, from whom it came, is offered, in reverent humility, this work, to swell, though never so feebly, that great Anthem which ever goeth up to him from all His Creation—that great Hymn He singeth back to Himself through all His works, to lull His Sabbaths to rest.

UNIVERSITY OF THE SOUTH,

SEWANEE, *June 9th*, 1875.

The following Review of the MS. of "THE SILVER WEDDING," by Dr. JOHN B. ELLIOTT, Professor of the Exact Sciences in the University of the South, is so chaste in style, and enters into such a thorough analysis of this work, that the author has sought and obtained Professor ELLIOTT's *permission to append it here as a Supplementary Preface.*

REVIEW of the MS. of "The Silver Wedding,"
by Dr. John B. Elliott, Professor of the Exact
Sciences, in the University of the South.

———————

THE SILVER WEDDING.

No work can be rightly judged unless fully
comprehended. For this reason we think "The
Silver Wedding" will meet with much adverse
criticism from those who, in a hasty reading, seek only
for the pleasures of sense. The poetry of its plan is
fathomed only after careful study; while the moral
of the poem in its highest application, depends upon
an understanding of its peculiar philosophy.

The work is essentially a unit. It cannot be
taken to pieces and criticised in detail without doing
at once injustice to the author and to the conception
which he embodies. Its constructive merit lies in
the connection between a legendary symbol and its
development in the main poem. The legend is a
key-note, the poem is the full sonata; they echo

and re-echo throughout the entire work, closing at
last in a full and final accord.

This is, nevertheless, but a bald statement of the
case.   To give a just idea of the work as a unit, a
detailed description of its construction must be
entered into.   The main poem is divided into five
separate parts, as follows : I. *At Home;* II. *Library
and Larder;* III. *Teraphim;* IV. *In Memoriam;*
V. *The Gifts.*   Through these five parts, run hand in
hand, the Legend and the Poem.   The Legend is
laid in the sunset days of King Arthur's court; in
those dark days when upon the grand old king began
to dawn the "loathsome opposite of all" his "heart
had destined;" when the fair, false Guinevere had
already sown the seed of that sad cry, wrung from
her by the king's forgiveness :—

> " Ah my God,
> " What might I not have made of thy fair world
> " Had I but loved thy highest creature here ! "

and heard already echoed in her heart, the " Late,
too Late " of the little maid's refrain.

During one day of feasting and mirth in this
degenerate court, transpire the judgments embodied

in the Legend. Like the main poem it, too, is divided into five parts, each one of which precedes and stands as a symbol for the corresponding part in the poem. Thus, the *Dwarf* precedes and symbolizes *At Home;* the *Boar's Head, and Knife* precede and symbolize *Library and Larder;* while *The Mantle, The Gold Wrought Horn,* and *Tuagor,* precede and symbolize respectively the *Teraphim, In Memoriam,* and *The Gifts.* The main Poem, the celebration of a *Silver Wedding,* is laid in modern times. Each part of the main Poem is a picture of perfect love and happiness centred upon the moral of the *Legend* as a study. As we glance at the fulness of the conception as embodied in the work, we can see in the degenerate court a symbol of a fallen world; in the Dwarf a judge; in Sir Cradocke and his "Ladie fair" the remnant of the faithful, while in the main poem we catch that strain of happiness, which awaits the good, through love made perfect.

The connection between the Legend and the Poem is made more close by Sir Cradocke of the Legend, symbolizing Bran Cradocke of the Poem;

this identity of names seeming intended to partially confuse, and thus to provoke interest and enquiry. The unity of the plan is not entirely fathomed until part fifth is reached. The author does, nevertheless, teach us by the different style and diction of the two parts that the poem is dual, and that the one in its simplicity and brevity is but the germ of the other. In the Legend the diction is terse and often abrupt. It seems designed to represent the undeveloped language of the legendary age, and takes us back to the days when *subject* and *object* were deemed the most important constituents of sentences. In the Poem the measure and diction is more flowing and elaborate, more modern. Here, in passing, we make a plea with our author for more liberality in future in the use of pronouns and articles in such expressions as the following, from the Legend :—

> " But some eat, only palate to cheat,"
> " Nor any failure now I dread,"
> " Quoth Sir Cradocke.   And Boar's head."
> He carved all true——"

While making such suggestions we nevertheless realise that our poet is intentionally "fighting back" from the sugar-sweet flow of modern verse to the rugged simplicity of the older writers. Still such reforms should rather be the gradual result of successive modifications. Much the same intention is shown in the versification; the quality of the work being hinted at in the metrical difference of the two parts. Against the "rhythm of arithmetical syllables and feet" war is declared, and the versification is based upon the "rhythm of accents." The author takes his stand expecting adverse criticism, but nevertheless, is bold in courting it, if so be he may maintain intact the full capabilities of English verse. This we deem will need no defence as long as Milton's verse is admired.

Such is the least we can say concerning the method and manner—the plan and structure of the work. Its aim and purpose can only be caught through a right understanding of the philosophy upon which the Poem rests. We have this philosophy shadowed forth in the preface in a translation of a portion of the *Third Hymn of Synesius*, presenting a symbol of the *Incarnation*. In relation to this our author adds that in such language we may in a secondary sense suppose the soul "addressing itself, through its union with God, as a duality, with the Higher Christian Pantheism of St. Paul." Passing for a moment from our author's philosophy to the criticism of an expression, we would take exception to the term *Higher Christian Pantheism*, not for any objectionable meaning implied in this place, but simply for its general uselessness. Christianity has no need for it, and gains nothing by the use of a term that is generally used in an anti-christian sense. Christian Pantheism is Theism. In another portion of the same hymn of Synesius, given by our author from Coleridge, it is made plain that the pantheism of Synesius is Spinozism, but with much more in addition. The "*One and all*" of Spinozism is supplemented by the "*One of all*," and the "*One and before all*," which, complementing Spinozism, raises it to Christian Theism. Admitting the seeming convenience of the expression "Higher Christian Pantheism" as intended to intensify and broaden conceptions conveyed by the expression "Christian

Theism," we nevertheless deprecate its use as tending to cast out an older expression which should be understood to embrace it. But, as we have said, we are criticising an expression and not our poet's philosophy. This latter includes all that the objectionable expression may mean in its highest sense, with rather an original application of its own. This peculiar application or interpretation of Christian Theism is the key-note of the work.

> " The All builds all thro' quest of mate to mate."
> " Know sex for object-subject."
> "————built through strife
> "————of like-unlike, or sex,
> " Self complemental.—"

are expressions which, with many others of like nature, we find running through the warp and woof of the poem. We do not think that we transcend the author's conception when we run this refrain of like-unlike back to the spiritual union of the *sinless* with the *sinful*, and see in the spiritual redemption of mankind, the great type of all creative union. We have in the incarnation (the spiritual reproduction, or redemption, of the spiritual all by the *all*), the type

of the production of the physical *all* by the inter-
action of the physical "like-unlike" "through quest
of mate to mate." Enlightened by this idea, the
high moral of the poem breaks upon us. Between
the purely spiritual ideal of "like-unlike" acting for
man's redemption, and the purely physical idea of
"male-female" throughout organic reproduction,
stands *man*, in whom the two combine. Destined
by the eternal plan to multiply through "quest of
mate to mate," as do all beneath him in the scale of
being, he yet contains within him that spiritual
element through which the marriage tie, as God-
ordained, becomes a sacred and holy thing. Such
we conceive to be the moral and the purpose of the
work. A noble conception, successfully fulfilled.

In regard to the general treatment of the subject
we must grant to our author the true crown of the
poet; He maketh all things new. He has given
us in a setting—rugged, many will say—but nevertheless brilliant, the never-fading jewel of Ideal Purity.
Through the joy and the tears of the *Silver
Wedding* we see its radiant flash and feel its worth.

The simple story lifts us from our moral turpitude to gaze upon what we *should be* as integral parts of that universe which has its beginning and end in the everlasting I AM. In these days of Mechanical Atheism and Dynamical Pantheism we say to all such works, " God speed." They point us past these incomplete philosophies to that high home above the dust, the strife, the wrong, where, born on poets' wing, we sometime dream we touch and rest, dwelling for a lightning's-flash in the nameless *Peace of God*.

JNO. B. ELLIOTT, M.D.,
Prof. Chem.

The reviews following, by the Professor of English Literature and the Professor of Theology, having been received, are added to that preceding; and having also received a note from a lady who had borrowed the MS. of " The Silver Wedding," the author cannot refrain from enclosing it herewith, valuing it as the opinion of an intelligent and well-read woman.

REVIEW of "The Silver Wedding," by Professor R. Dabney, Professor of English Literature and Metaphysics.

———— ————

This work is a hymn to the spirit of Love as exhibited in all the realms of nature, giving coherence and unity to the whole plan. God, as himself one, has created his universe to contain, in all its variety, an essential unity; and the correspondence of part to complementary part is as necessary to the conservation as to perpetuation of nature. This spirit of unity is Love, or like seeking like though unlike.

It is this thought, this conception, that runs through the whole piece, giving to it its form, its tone and its colouring. As it treats of essential unity in apparent duality, the poem is itself an essential unit in a dual form: the Legend and the Silver Wedding running parallel until they converge in the conclusion and bend into one; harmonious; like though unlike; complementary, the one to the other. The one is an ancient legend; the other its modern correlative exhibiting that the same spirit pervades ancient and modern alike. Not only does this spirit pervade all time, but it pervades all space; and the details of the poem are an application of this idea of correspondence to the facts of nature; that there is a marriage unity in all the works of God, mental and physical, animate and inanimate, organic and inorganic, in the winds and the waves, in the sun and the moon and the starry hosts, in joy and in sorrow, in the Ariel and the Caliban that are in man, in Christ and His church, in God and His universe. It would carry us much beyond our limits to trace the correspondences of part to complementary part as exhibited, described and exemplified in the work; but its form and its structure savour of it throughout. It is exhibited in the double form of the work itself; described in the course of the narrative and the detail of the poem; exemplified in the imagery and verse; all conspiring in their complex multiformity to produce a unitized impression on the mind. The unity is not a simple classic but a complex Gothic one; indeed, there is much of the gothic spirit breathing through the work: and, though complete in itself, it may well be but a part of a larger and a grander whole. It is this unity of correspondency that gives shape to the poem, measure to the verse, coherence to the imagery, and language to the thought.

The recognition of these correspondences, this dualunity of nature, material and spiritual, as a philosophic fact, is capable of being stated in a didactic poem and discussed as a philosophic question; but, imaged under the representation of love and marriage, it obtains a poetic interest, without, however, losing its philosophic import. Thus it is, that the poem treating of such a problem may, in all strictness, be called a philosophic poem, not in the sense of mere didactic truths cramped into verse, as in Pope's "Essay on Man," but imaged to the mind in true ideal or poetic style. It is this power to discern and appreciate the internal beauty of the

universe, which makes poetry a perennial stream
not confined within geographical limits, but flowing
through all lands, fertilising and beautifying God's
footstool and rejoicing the heart of man ; not indi-
genous to certain stages of intellectual development
or degrees of civilisation.   Of the poetic import of
the universe we would say, as was said of truth—

"The eternal years of God are hers."

In fact, the poetic is the ideal true; in the
words of Mr. Carlyle,—"The writer should betake
himself, with such faculty as he has, to understand
and record what is true.   Poetry, it will come
more to be understood, is nothing but higher knowledge and the only romance (for grown persons),
Reality."   If we do not mistake this is more and
more becoming the poetic creed of the modern
school.   External nature in its outward forms is
the centre and circumference of Scott's poetry ;
passion is the deity which reigns in Byron's ; but
intellectual insight, the power to discern and appreciate the internal harmonies of the universe, "the
sense sublime" of the "spirit" "rolling through all

things " is the spirit of Wordsworth's lofty rhyme. This style is pushed to its extreme by Mr. Tennyson, of whose school, it is evident, the author is. The language of the legend is very Tennysonian. He is evidently a zealous devotee of the Poet Laureate, who is no democrat in letters, but writes for the initiated, and does not " carry his secret on his sleeve."

Differences there may and will be about how the author has performed his work; but, for that he has spoken a *true* word of how God's universe has imaged itself to his mind, and that he has *truly* recorded what he has seen in it; we gratefully accept it, and regard it as a worthy offering on the shrine of *truth*. As a whole, we esteem it as a work of much merit; and besides telling its own story, it shows the writer to be a man of deep sensibility, permeated with the spirit of melodious thought.

To be fully appreciated, it requires more thought than can be reasonably expected from the casual reader, who reads to be amused, or to fill up the vacancy of an idle hour; for him this poem was not written.

REVIEW by Rev. Dr. Du Bose, Professor of Theology
in the University of the South.

THE SILVER WEDDING.

THE writer of this notice regrets that he can only
record the impressions left upon his mind by a rapid
and single reading of the above-named Poem; and
that, after so long a time as renders it impossible
to give an account of the causes to which the
impression is due.

It is some months since, overcoming a strong
reluctance to examining literary, and especially
poetical, matter in MS., he sat down not over
willingly nor hopefully to the perusal of the " Silver
Wedding." He had been requested, as he now in
turn takes the liberty of requesting others, to read
the poem through, if possible at a sitting, and to
suspend judgment until it can be judged of as a

whole. As he himself thus sat and read he imperceptibly lost all note of time ; and when at last he rose and laid down the book, as unwillingly as he had taken it up, there was a spell upon him similar in kind and only inferior in degree to that exerted over him fifteen years before by Tennyson's Idyls. But this impression was only the gradual result of continuous reading. It was only by degrees that his not over poetical ear, trained only in Tennyson's subtle and perfect music, fell into the unusual and not always smooth and easy rhythmical movement of the verse. Still more it was only by degrees that his mind scaled the heights and sounded the depths of the profound philosophy which finds here an utterance for itself, and constitutes, perhaps, the serious purpose of the poem.

The author is through and through Tennysonian; and yet at the same time just as thoroughly individual. He is the opposite of an imitator. He is intensely original, so intensely original that his very faults are so a part of himself that one sees not how they can be separated from him. His work not only comes from himself, it *is* himself. And it does not choose for itself a form; it *makes* for itself a form, by an inward necessity and law of its own.

This is true both of his poetry and of his philosophy. In the latter especially, he cannot use at second hand the cut and dried phraseology of the school. His thought must mould its own forms; in consequence of which he is not easily understood by those who are tied to the language of the schools. To understand him, one must enter into his mind and understand his words, not as the text book understand them, but as *he* understands them.

But he is Tennysonian inasmuch as he is poet-interpreter of those elements in our nature, which have found voice and utterance, first, perhaps, in Wordsworth, but fully and completely only in him, to whom we do homage as Poet Laureate, not only of England but of the English-speaking world. The passions are developed in all, and the poetry of the passions is comprehensible to all. The school of Tennyson gives voice to something in us higher than our passions—that better part which is *not* developed

in all, and the language of which is not intelligible
to all. In it we find utterances for those subtler,
finer, higher elements of our nature, which need to
be cultivated in order that they may be known to
exist, and the language of which, therefore, is comprehensible only to the cultivated few. The soul
craves something above the mere gratification of
earthly passions. It throws out delicate tendrils
into the unknown that lies beyond the sphere of
sense, and seeks to lay hold of and cling to the
Infinite and the Eternal. Earthly love like that of
Sir Cradocke—or the more modern Bran Cradocke—
purged from all earthly impurity and assimilated to the
Divine love : or, higher still, love like Sir Galahad's,
lifted above the earth and earthly objects and made
divine : earthly love purified, love purifying itself
above the earthly and rising into the heavenly—
these are the themes of this purest of all our schools of
poetry. And this is the theme of this poem, the puri-
fication of love, until human love become again in the
end that which it was in the beginning, one with the
divine love, and man and God become One in love.

DEVOIR.

———

Place aux Dames !—

Aux Dames du moyen âge

Place d'honneur !

———

CONTENTS.

THE PROLOGUE.

THE PROLOGUE.

Lord God of Light, almighty Word,
    When thro' the void reverberate
With Thy grand loneliness, was heard
    Nor speech, nor sound, of aught create:
Thy Thought from that dread silence spoke—
    "Let there be light:" and there was light:
Light! instant Light! and then awoke
    Thy Power all-creative, bright,
Refresht in Thine own beams, to build
    The All thro' light, and heat, the bride
Of light; thro' married rays that gild
    With beauty, or secluse, do hide,

To warm, and nourish, and cherish, anew,
  The All from Thee to being, whorled
Light! male and female light, which two
  Great sexes animate the world,
Stored in each orb.* Lord of Light,
  Almighty Thought, Word, Power, Deed,
Who from on High, thy place of might,
  Thy humblest deignest still to heed
That work thy works, though lowest cell,
  Bacterium, or sparrow's fall,
Or lily bloom'd thy power to tell
  In lowly beauty ; Lord, to all,
Thy Light is rayed to wake the song
  Of being and work, all have, from Thee,
To sing Thy praise—Deign, Thou, that wrong,
  Untruth, mar not my minstrelsy."

Thus I, as seeking help : to sing
  A theme mysterious, yet plain

---

* Milton. See Title-page motto.

And homely ; reaching furthest ring

   And verge of planet to blend its strain

With spheral harmonies ; yet voiced,

   Low-voiced, from the nursery

Of human mother, or all rejoiced

   For saving birth, triumphantly,

In song of the Virgin Mother.   Nay,

   A theme of All, building the All,

Thro' quest of mate to mate : the day

   Of all existence sped in thrall

Of male and female light : thro' will

   Of God, Creator ; yet, Himself

Wed with humanity ; while, still,

   Begotten Son of Man, Himself

The only begotten Son of God,

   God humbled to humanity,

And made to kiss the Father's rod,

   To set his earthborn brothers free ;

God, wedded with humanity

   To bless the All to lowest molds :

And since the highest, humanity,
 The type of all the rest enfolds,
Made in His image ; so in bond
 Of God-join'd human pair is type
And blessing whole and round,
 When is a generation-cycle ripe :
And this I sought for help to sing
 Of light, male and female, shedding
A lifetime glory: this theme to sing—
 The Symbol of the Silver-Wedding.

For, on a winter's evening, one,
 A friendly visitor, my room
Had left ; and left me there alone
 When winter's darkening evening gloom,
Made cheerful by a glowing hearth,
 Invited musing on our talk :
Which all was on the sterling worth,
 And life-tried virtues, and daily walk,

Of a married pair, much valued friends,

    Whose Silver-Wedding, the eve before,

We both, with throng of other friends,

    Had sought to crown with honour more,

And with a difference of renown,

    Than ever Silver-Wedding gained :

And my companion, now just gone,

    Was he who thus my song constrained

To sing the Silver-Wedding.   He

    Full well this worthy pair had known

Throughout their lives, and came to see

    Their second nuptials ; came to own,

As spokesman for the rest, their worth,

    And all there, known were well, to him ;

Though, save his name, unknown his birth ;

    And he was aged ; and shrunk in limb ;

Though bright and keen his eye.   And some

    The younger folk—so aged was he,

Irreverent said he first had come

    When all began, and so would be

Till all had ending.   Men and times
   He seem'd to know as one whose eye,
On manners, customs, of all climes
   And every age, had look'd ; to die
Not doom'd, it seem'd indeed.   He told
   Of all their youth ; their married life ;
How five-and-twenty years had roll'd
   Around to wed again true man and wife,
Bringing them honours from the past,
   To crown the worthy pair esteem'd
Of all the worthiest.   And his talk,
   As is the way of elders, teem'd
With anecdote ; with ancient saws
   Re-set with modern instance : nay
He even told, to show the laws
   Unchanged that human nature sway,
A Legend of an olden time
   Grown dim beyond the centuries
Confusing all, save but for rhyme,
   As walking men and trees.

But told as though himself had seen
    Whereof he told. '' Translate,'' he said,
'' And blend truth old, with new—I mean
    Old truth renew to bridle the led,
Rash, foaming steeds of Progress, fretting
    To break away. Much is wrong
With Progress, thro' flimsy harness, setting
    On new departures forth on long
And weary, doubtful way that wends
    Throughout the ages. Put old wine
Into new bottles ; and though ends
    The journey only on dividing line
Between eternity and time ;
    And though the wine be drawn from cask
Forgotten, cobwebbed, from its prime
    Of vintage cellar'd, your task
Shall have reward : for put old wine
    Into bottles new, and none shall break :
And truth renewed is truth divine,
    Etern the thirst of soul to slake.

Hear even your great thinker* call

   To kindle the sacred fire anew

On th' altar smouldering, yet not all,

   Though well-nigh, quench'd for want of true

Enlivening zeal of vital faith :

   ' For faith makes us, and not we it,

Makes its own forms ' with truth he saith.

   I know on heart of time is writ

' The faith delivered to the saints

   Once and for all time.'   Other truth,

The thinker utters—nay sun paints

   This truth on ripened fruit, in ruth

As for its fall, to earth drawn down

   With seed enwombed for birth from death ;

To glory, from dishonour, sown ;

   Raised from humility ; by breath

Of vernal breezes fanned in warm

   And gladding sunlight,—again to be.

---

* Emerson.

Yea, true it is, attract and charm

 Of gravitation, and purity,

Purity of heart, have lode

 In one identic law concluse

Whereby the All shall see its God,

 Come home to Him again to fuse

Into His will. For attract and law

 Of gravitation are the Ought

And Conscience that all matter, draw

 To duty; and are one with Ought

And Conscience of the soul made pure,

 And making pure, thereby: one law

For both to make their orbit sure,

 Lest free-will, free-play, from orbit draw:

One law, only differentiate

 As may the object-subject be:

For Spirit, Matter, are perturbate—

 Nay, of the All-machinery,

What, but working-loose, is free-will,

 Of universe the wear and tear,

D

Allowed, yet needing the maker's skill
    And watchful, overruling care,
With Progress much is wrong, my friend,"
    Continued he—" much every way.
And now reaction seeks to mend
    The broken cisterns of the day :
Disgust begins to ask what mean
    These wild, vain beatings of the air ?
Wherefore on help of leaders lean
    Who lend support to lead nowhere,
Save as the blind do lead the blind ?
    Under the sun *is* nothing new
But change, yea ceaseless change, to bind
    Anew the old to work the true,
Unchanging will of God. *I* know,"
    Said he—" have seen, before this day,
Much wrong with progress thro' the throe
    Of wabbling* free-will : and this say

---

    * See Webster's " Unabridged Dictionary " for definition of
this word.

Of ill to Progress—well-nigh its worst
    That much is wrong with man and wife.
But hope the better : the sun hath burst,
    Ere now, from clouds to sweeten life
And free from mould and gnawing rust.
    Translate the Legend : the time is meet,
Grows weary of the praise of lust
    And wandering fires ; and longs for seat
Once more beside enduring glow
    Of purer hearth and home.   Now pray
Permit me," said he rising,—" no,"
    When I would him longer stay,
" With thanks, no, ye repute me old,
    And so must I pass on my way.
Being old, I hear the compline toll'd,
    Being old, pass on to end my day."
And passed he on so quietly,
    That scarce I missed his going out.
For left alone, it seemed to me
    His voice still stayed with me and wrought

In converse ; blending yet its tones
　　With mine own musing as before
The fire I sat, and with the moans
　　Of winter's wind that, as night wore
Past twilight, thro' the casement sighed
　　And whisper'd of the coming strife
Of storm and darkness.　Nor belied
　　The wind its tidings : for soon rife
Was night with storm, and rose the fray
　　Crescend to full diapason or fell
Shaking, trembling, to die away,
　　As mighty organ-volumed swell.
And anon the chimney in assonance
　　Was resonant with the storm-chords
And from a smouldering quiet, as dance
　　Imprison'd flames in tubes to words
Or notes of song, the fire would leap
　　With upward spring, and flare
With sudden light, and shadows heap
　　On wall, and shapes, that in the glare

Pass'd soon to shades dissolved in turn,

   As were the visions seen in glow

Of coals.   And musing thus, in turn

   Myself would seem, in thought, to know

Myself as though I were, yet seem

   To be not, save as might be merged

My being in the All in dream

   Of reverie.   And sounds, as surged

Or fell the storm, around the room,

   Were mingled with my reverie,

And a great music as the gloom

   And night shook with the harmony

Of spheral chords all bright with light

   And grand with majesty, and sweet

With faith and trust in love and might

   Of the All-Father, from th' All with heat

And light working His works and singing

   To Him a hymn of being and praise.

Also, 'twas as though the wind came bringing

   Out from the night, as from days

Long past, yet present, voices speaking
   Thro' window, as of human joys
And sorrows ; and of trials reeking
   With sweat of struggle ; of base alloys,
Yet of pure gold in human life :
   Household voices of hearth and home,
Of homely ways, of man and wife,
   And voices of gleeful children ; of groom
And maid that serve the hearth.
   Nor did quaint humour want a voice,
Nor even homely flippant mirth,
   Chattering, as homestead birds rejoice.

And ever and anon came still
   The voice of mine ancient friend
Telling his Legend : came still
   Ever and anon unto the end.

AT HOME.

THE LEGEND.

THE DWARF.

I.

Three merrier days in merry Carleile
Saw never Arthur's court, the while
For festival in month of May,
When king and Table Round would stay
For rest of careless joyance there
In merrie Carleile, with ladies fair:
Careless, all, ladie and knight;
Careless, save of joust, and might
In tourney shown with splintered lance,
Or conquest gained, in hall, thro' glance
Of amorous loose, gay dalliance:

Careless, all, of name or fame ;

Careless all, both knight and dame ;

Thoughtless, all, on God, or saint :

The Sanct Dubrece made sore complaint.

II.

Who, holy man, archbishop, he

Sometime of rich Carleon's see,

Would crozier yield, and a hermit be.

And he it was who sang, I ween,

The sacred service when the queen,

His second queen, king Arthur wed,

Meeting her, to altar led,

Crowned and robed right royally ;

Attended there most loyally ;

By five fair other royal dames,

(Of Arthur's escort-kings the wives,

In precedence, had they, their names),

They dames all fair, of fairest lives,

Each bearing in hand a snow-white dove,

Nor ever any light of love,

As never in his first queen's reign,

Known then in Arthur's court; nor bane

From scandal's fang; nor could there be,

With men all brave, and women free

From all reproach : and all men knew,

Knew Arthur's court the purest, best,

In Christendom—all brave, all true,

Yet in Caerleon might not rest

The Sanct Dubrece; archbishop, he

His see would yield, and a hermit be.

III.

For he bethought him of the feast,

How toiled for pleasure man and beast,

So long before by night and day,

To make a three days feast : how they

Began provision long before,

As if might last for evermore,

A three days feast : then much more wise,

Thought he, than perishing greed to prize
To seek eternal joys to gain
In heaven—thro' prayer, and fast, and pain,
And so, the Sanct Dubrece his see
And crozier would leave ; would hermit be
And dwell in cell, in a lone countrée.

IV.

The years they came, the years they went
And Sanct Dubrece, beyond Caergwent,
In prayer and miracle, there still dwelt ;
Him, fast and scourge, full well he delt,
His life, thro' zeal, now well-nigh spent.
And Guinever the Fair, the good,
Entombed near Glastonbury Rood,
Was 'tween two pyramids interred ;
Where Arthur, dead, with her shall be ;
And in her place, another stood
As Arthur's queen. And she, the third,
Was also Guinever—ay me,

Disdainful, fairest, falsest, she—

Beautiful in frailtie.

v.

And thro' the land was cried aloud

The sin of Guinever the Proud,

With Lancelot, the king's best knight,

With Arthur's chiefest friend.   And light

Of baleful beauty shot out sin

And all the land was filled with sin

Thro' her : and bruit thereof struck knell

Of woe on Sanct Dubrece his cell,

And tolled a dirge in scorn and shame :

For careless were all of name or fame ;

Careless, all, both knight and dame ;

Thoughtless, all, on God or saint :

And Sanct Dubrece made sore complaint.

vi.

And fasted he, the more and more,

And prayed he, then all the more,

And scourged him for evermore,

For sins not his, the holy man,

That so might he with heaven prevail,

And turn away the wrath and ban,

Of heaven and holy saints, from frail

And sinful flesh.   To Our Lady mild,

And to fair Christ our Lord, her child,

The Sanct Dubrece in sore distress

Made sore complaint, and did confess

For sins not his, to make redress.

VII.

But he this mercie only gained,

Of heavenly dole for him so pained,

That could, sans doubt, one pair be found

Of Arthur's court and Table Round,

One only pair therein be found,

Doughty knight with ladie fair,

True knight, and ladie chaste as fair,—

That, then, should stay the day of doom,

From Arthur's court and Table Round
And all the land ; until fair room
Of penitence had they, a space :
And this the Sanct obtained, thro' grace,
As boon from heaven in ruth for this,
His prayer and penance for sins not his.

VIII.

And that might he be certain made,
(Too hard should else such knowledge be),
Was power given the Sanct, in aid
Of doubtful search, unseen, unbade,
To stand in midst of all around,
Until he willed their eyes unbound,
As if by conscience loosed to see,
A dwarf misshapen ; to make them dree
The sting of conscience, yet not know
This blessing, from Sanct Dubrece, to flow.

IX.

He, holy man, of humble mind,

Would only to heaven his good deeds show—

But them would help their sins to find,

Thro' spell of sacred magic gifts,

Which—like as conscience bares the soul,

With probing touch explores the whole,

And secret sin to judgment lifts—

Might test in Arthur's court the fame

Of careless knight, of careless dame,

And do away their sin thro' shame

And grief of unfeigned penitence

For evil wrought thro' carnal sense.

X.

Three merrier days in merrie Carleile

Saw never Arthur's court the while

That Guinever the third, his queen,

And court of dames the fairest seen,

Kept festival in flowering May,

When king and Table Round would stay,

For rest of careless joyance there,

In merrie Carleile with ladies fair.

XI.

The third May day, the Beltine fires—

Fit token of evil that Baal inspires

In heart consumed with its own desires,

Still smouldered on with ash-quenched brand:

The third day, played, were still all games—

The forelost battle, fought flowers in hand,

Of winter to summer, by youthful band ;

At landmarks, flogged to mark the site,

Breeched urchins writhed in useful despite ;

Thro' church-roof dropped, wood-devil was beat.

The fleshly devil not thus they treat,

But only seek the devil to cheat :

And Sanct Dubrece heard devilrie,

From court to hamlet in revelrie.

XII.

To the third day feast, Sir Quex* did call
The court to gather in the great hall;
Small reverence had he, for any and all
At banquet hour, this seneschall:
So king and court left off their maying,
Uncaring to vex Sir Quex, delaying,
His ordinal of feast; and all
The court was gathered in hall,
And stand in groups therein around,
Till Prelude of the Salt should sound;—
There, Yvain,—Eric,—Caravis,—
Cligés,—the handsome unknown, Coedis,—
Lancelot, the mightiest knight,
Whose sin with Guinever brought blight
Upon the land and Table Round.—
Sir Jaufre, Sir Cologranant, Sir Kay,

---

* Sir Quex in Armorica, Sir Kay in Britain.

Sir Gawain stronger to fight than pray ;
There, all his knights the king surround,—
All but few : all gathered there,
In his great hall, with ladies fair.

XIII.

When, in their midst, they know not how,
A Dwarf is seen, where none ere now
Saw aught but empty space.   And stilled,
Is all their converse gay, thro' dread :
As if some power unknown had willed
Their eyes to see one from the dead,
As if a conscience, there they saw,
A dwarf misshapen : come to draw
Their sins to trial before its law.

XIV.

A Dwarf, in sooth, misshapen he :
Uncouth, unkempt, him would they flee,
But may not from his gaze escape :
Each feels his every sin unsafe

Before that searching eye.   In sooth,

Was he misshapen dwarf; nor ruth

Was any in his austere mien :

So unwelcome guest was never seen.

Of wrinkled hardness, all his face,

Is seamed with sore-red fissures deep ;

His eyelids, swollen as with long sleep,

Wallow, swine in bushy lair ;

An inky flood, his unkempt hair ;

His shoulders drooped, his spine an hump,

His back doth bear a grievous lump;

His trembling hands do pick at mote,

Or clutch at stains on ragged coate,--

For ragged his coate, with many a stain,

As of one long among potsherds lain :

A Dwarf, in sooth, misshapen he,

Uncouth, unkempt, unwishen to see

At court : so would they flee this shape,

But may not from its gaze escape.

XV.

For that grim Dwarf had an eye of fire
Which burned thro' mail or any attire
That cloaked a sin ; and fiercer flamed
Thereafter, or to duller tamed,
As might be they on whom it turned,
As testing thus what sort it burned—
And turned on Lancelot, the knight
Became as one who, wrestling, might
Gone mad with violent remorse,
Seek heaven to take by stormy force—
Berserker in repentance, he ;
And fiercely blazed the Dwarf's eye then.
Next on the queen it fell, and she
Became as one who might from ken
Of world—sore stricken with soul blame,
From her high place of pride, in shame
Might grovel low at Arthur's feet,
Her fair hair loosed, at Arthur's feet,

Clasped by her fair hands;* as is meet,

When come the doom her sin had earned ;

But still, in all humility

Laid low, might she an abbess be :

But now the Dwarf's eye radiant burned,

And shot out blaze of baleful beautie,

Radiant blaze of baleful beautie,

Haught with pride :—so, fiercely flamed,

Or sank, to sullen dulness tamed,

As might be on whom the Dwarf's eye turned,

As testing thus what sort it burned.

XVI.

Not there was Enid : she, I trow,

Proud young mother, had gone to show

At Iniol's castle, her young Geraint—

From sparrow-hawk there now no constraint—

As pledged her mother by Prince Geraint,

When he to court would Enid bear,

* Guinever: Tennyson.

In her faded silk she erst did wear :

Not in the great hall was Enid that day,

Else had the Dwarf's eye beamed with ray

All tender, firm, and pure.   Not there,

Sir Galahad : he gone was where

He seemed, past burning bridges* afar,

To Percivale, a silver star :

Else had the Dwarf's Eye surely dazed

All beholding, through sheen that blazed

With diamond royalties of crown

That one should crown him with afar.

Nor was Percivale at court that day ;

And others a few were still away :—

But, when the Dwarf eyed Gawain,—down,

Down to earth, slantwise with frown,

The Dwarf's eye, lurid flashing first,

Sunk paled, to earth ; as when the burst

Of shooting star athwart the sky

Pales aslant to fall and die,

---

* Holy Grail.

In earth air, quenched; and the knight,

Sir Gawain, became as one who might,

For doom, his soul, as if wandering star,

Well know,—wandering near and far,

That ever to earth seeks to repair,

To quench in nothingness of air

Its luridness fresh-lit from Tophet.

To Gawain, the Dwarf is judge and prophet,—

And to all the rest, I ween—

This uncouth Dwarf, with gaze so keen:

This unkempt Dwarf with the eye of fire,

Which burned thro' mail, or any attire,

That cloaked a sin. And all do chafe:

Each feels his every sin unsafe:

But of his kingly mind to know this thing,

With kingly calm, then quoth the king :—

XVII.

" Sir Dwarf, Sir Dwarf! speak,—whence art
　　thou ?
Surely, not here, wert thou ere now."
" Lord Arthur, wherefromever I be,
Know, surely, stand I here with ye ;
And wherefore come, shall soon all see."

———————————

THE SILVER WEDDING.

THE SILVER WEDDING.

PART I.

AT HOME.

I.

DECEMBER's evening air, with frosty cold,
Was freshening fast.   The evening sun, grown old
With the waning year, yet hale and ruddy, sent
His beams to hang the golden shields, whose glint
From mullion'd windows of a house—of stone,
Grey, ivy-clad—gave token then that One
A watch had set o'er those who therein dwelt,
Against the darkness creeping through the gloaming;
Until the orient Sun, refresh'd from roaming
Throughout the Blessed Isles, again should melt

The morning mists.   The cheerful, married blaze
Of vestal hearths with houselights, streamed a haze
In warmer tints upon the bluish damps
Of evening; and the many-colour'd lamps,
That buoyed out the winding carriage way,
From lodge and open gate to ivied porch,
Shined out a light—for Silver Wedding torch—
Of hospitable welcome on a lingering day,
Whose winter Sun shone on a Silver Wedding
Of time-tried lovers: their roof-tree, this peaceful
     steading.

II.

The North-west Wind swept clear the avenue;
The North-west Wind the road begins to strew
With leaves of oak and chestnut, brown in hue;
Leaves, in the hollows, garner'd by the Wind,
The Wind uncovers now from thatch of snow,
And leaves, few leaves, still waiting left behind.
From sapless trees the Wind—not all unkind
The North-west Wind that now begins to blow—

Now culls to join again: as if to show

A chastened warp and woof of life, laid down

To carpet the way, when friends the wedding crown.

The Sun gone down, and the silver starlights hung,

High twinkling, from blue-frescoed depths of heaven,

Upon this Silver Wedding of a pair who clung

Thro' life, God join'd, with love that naught had riven,

Nor man, nor clash of will, nor disaster's leaven.

III.

Their home, this dwelling rear'd of massy stone

Built honestly: of stone whose quarried blue

Time's touch had soften'd down to grey—of tone

Mellowed into exceeding richness, thro' the hue

Of russet iron-mould, reliev'd with myriad scales

Of glist'ning mica,—when the Summer Sun,

Wearied with brassy skies and a hot day's run,

At evening seeks to bathe his glowing rays

Where the ivy's cool and winding green embays,

In eddying course among the sloping vales

Of roofs steep-gabled, and mountainous with slate;

Or drowns the porch, or round the oriel high,

In leafy streamlet flows.   Nor Autumn late,

Nor harsh Winter, the chasten'd charm abate:

Autumn—steel-graving lines in sober phase

Varied of silver-grey; those shades—*and sigh*—

Of still, grey harmony of th' Unreal loom'd

With Real, upon the landscape broadly gloom'd,

Yet clear-cut in scene, aglow with red-leaf blaze,

Very present, actual, visible, but all shut out

From work-day world, from daily work-day rout,

And shading dreamily—dreamily—into haze,

And background ever deepening in the maze,

Toward Eternity—yet faith the maze

Shall pierce, and thro' clear depths of heaven know

That, still, beyond, dwells God.*   And when the hand

Of winter, cramp'd with cold, engraves the land

With icy lines and slanting strokes of snow,—

Falling noiseless, as tho' the earth to show,

---

* Sermon of the Bishop of Lincoln.

Mantled,—with gentle ruth, relenting care,

Against too harsh, deep etching film'd : when blare

And blast of mad Storm, who seeks the earth to bare,

Is heard ; or heard, his sighings as he dreams

Of toying,—oh with summer leaves long dead,—

And sleeps in tears, before still midnight gleams

With moonlight sparkling on the frozen snow :

When silent, busy Frost, with crunching tread,

Upon the crusting snow goes to and fro,

And maketh up, against the coming beams

Of morrow's Sun, the Lord's earth-jewels, then—

Full ! O Lord ! is earth of thy glory then !

Ah, then, from rising of that glorious sun.

Even to the going down in evening dun,—

And drear to Robin, who his ruddy breast

Against the window shows, and makes his quest

With fearless pecking, for snowbirds largess bidding

As for himself ; aye, then, each day--yea, night

And day—the soul of him, who the right

Of master over that grey house and steading,

F

Doth bless his God for pleasant lines, to him
And his, in pleasant places, fallen : to brim
Are fill'd his barns and store with plenty ; full
His heart ; and of his substance, he the poor
Gives large remembrance : beginning at his door
With Robin and hungry snowbirds : well he knows,—
Ah, Coleridge, may I ?—

"He prayeth best who loveth best
  All things both great and small ;
For the dear God who loveth us,
  He made and loveth all."

But, never, thankfulness, before, his heart,
With richer tribute fill'd, than when, this day,—
His Silver Wedding-day—he sat apart,
Alone.

IV.

Alone : although the library shows th' array
Of companionable walls, book-built ; with cunning
    art

In alcoves entrant and re-entrant, bastion'd :

Unparley'd ; by broom of housemaid, only, question'd ;

And warder'd by the book-spirits.   But these,

Even these, the silent ministers, faithful true,

Of quiet dear to those who love them, nor sees,

Nor heeds he, now : but drawn within, with view

All introspective, and perception dull

To outer touch his senses sought to cull,

From memory's garden (by association lock'd

Or opened), flowers of thought in beauty bloom'd ;

Fruits luscious with happiness—alas, too, some con-
 sumèd

With sorrow's canker : aye, some flowers mockèd

With premature decay, and faded, torn

From stem left bare and cruel with wounding thorn

Of sharp affliction.   Thus, alone, secluse,

The master of Graystead sat : nor discontent,

Nor jealousy, the gentle book-spirits feel

At his unwont neglect, but round him wheel,

In loving, silent guardianship, content

To serve in watchful quiet: as a recluse

Is oft, by angels watched in lonely cell,

Who reckons up his life, and tells his beads

In prayer, on mount afar from sound of bell,

And chant of singing monks, or voice that reads

The Golden Legend of saintly acts.

II.

THE LIBRARY AND LARDER.

THE LEGEND.

II.

THE BOAR'S HEAD AND KNIFE.

I.

OUTSPAKE Sir Quex :* "The feast doth wait"—

As rigid his, as rules of fate ;

Small reverence had he for any and all,

At banquet hour, this seneschal—

" The feast doth wait, doth lose its zest

When stayed by an unwelcome guest."

II.

Then Arthur : " Quex !—again ?—how long

Shalt thou my patience do such wrong,

---

* Quex in Armorica, Kaye in Britain.

And blurr our motto with thy cark ?

' Spread be my board'—to our motto hark—

As horizon, round; and ample be,

As heart, its hospitalitie ;

So all, nor first nor last, shall share it,

But equal all with equal merit.'*

Once more, Sir Quex, I bid thee hark,

And now, with reverence due, to mark,

The motto of our Table Round.

Bid prelude of the salt now sound,—

For merit enough this strange Dwarf hath

To make—save thee—all dread his scath."

" God speed thee, King Arthur ! and with the
      queen,

Thy fair queen Guinever, be seen

God's favour;—grant, I pray, me grace

To speak but three words, face to face,

With this thy seneschal," said then

The Dwarf.   Quoth Arthur: " Speak thy will !"

* The motto of the Round Table.

III.

The Dwarf then made Sir Quex to ken

Three words, spoken hard and shrill :—

" Behold thy feast ! "   And yellow light,

As if of molten metals bright,

The Dwarf's eye shone ; and then became

Sir Quex as one who stood in shame,

And was as tho' he saw the feast,

Thro' false purveyance, false, and least

For vouchered cost : all false the plate,

With baser metal and light weight,

False weight and measure, tho' outside fine ;

False the viands, false the wine ;

Falser when bought, tho' false in selling :

Thus on all the sin was telling,

Of Guinever, the proud, false fair ;

All, inside false, and outside fair :

And Quex, once honest, got sharp pain,

At Mammon's hands, thro' lust of gain.

IV.

And then, strange deed in sooth was wrought,

The Dwarf's eye burned the feast to naught.

Quoth Arthur, seeing Quex did chafe,—

" I know not if even my crown be safe.

But, Quex, thy feast hath molten down,

And now all dinnerless are we,

Whatever may betide our crown."

But said the Dwarf : " That may not be."

V.

And now was heard a nearing sound

Of hunter's horn and baying hound ;

And into hall, with panting roar,

Rushed in a bristling, tusked boar.

Sans fear, the Dwarf him caught to kill ;

And just as the boar lay stark and still,

Rode into the great hall,—a goodly sight !—

Sir Cradocke the Strong Arm'd, the Battle
    Knight,

Of the Three Battle Knights, was he ;
And with him rode his fair ladie.

VI.

"Pardon ! Sir Arthur, my lord and king,
Not I would so unseemély thing,
As fill your great and royal hall
With baying hounds and huntsman's call,—
Not of mine own will, free and clear ;
But power unknown hath forced me here,
With boar and hounds, and my ladie dear
With me ; else, so unseemély,
Hadst thou seen them not, nor me."
"Pardon," quoth Arthur, " have I none,
For him who ill hath never done."

VII.

Then drew the Dwarf a knife so keen,
That one blow severed the Boar's Head
    clean.

And none knew how, yet placed on dish,

Was the Boar's Head cooked as mouth could wish ;

And filled the hall with so savourie smell,

Never such hunger the court befel.

Then said Sir Cradocke : " My dear, dear dame,

Such savour from thy kitchen came

When last we slew a boar."   " And now,"

The Dwarf said, " only he, I trow,

Can carve this Boar's Head, he the strong,

Whose dame hath never done him wrong."

VIII.

Sore dismayed, there, many a knight ;

It seemed as if none carve it might ;

Some hid their knives, as tho' they'd none.

Ay me ! it seemed much wrong were done.

Then quoth the king : " If any here

May carve this Boar's Head without fear,

'Tis thou, Sir Cradocke, our strong-soul knight

May'st carve it true in this Dwarf's sight.

IX.

The Dwarf then at Sir Cradocke looked :

And the knight believes the Boar's Head cooked

In kitchen of his own dear dame.

The Dwarf next on the ladie looked,

As on her lord : and she became,

In beautie, as of the glorified :

For all the beautie of her youth,

And beautie of her faith well tried,

And all the beautie of her truth,

And all the beautie of her soul

That brought her scathless to this goal,

And all the beautie of her love

Uprose thro' form and face :

As when, at eve, comes on apace,

And spreads from earth through heaven, a bloom

Of the life above the evening's gloom,

Blushing thro' the evening's calm,

And soothes the soul with rose-red balm.

X.

In beautie of wife and womanhood,
Sir Cradocke's ladie before all stood ;
And well, I ween, Sir Cradocke will,
Ever thus behold her, still—
(Nor ever time, his sight shall dull)
For ever young and beautiful.

XI.

Then to the dame, that bright, keen knife,
The Dwarf did give. " How now, fair wife !—
Mine own good knife, is truly, this ;
With this, their laughter, nor their hiss,
Nor any failure, now I dread ! "—
Quoth Sir Cradocke. And Boar's Head,
He carved all true, with his own good knife
The Dwarf did give him, by his wife.
The king, this knight and dame, doth greet :
And cried the Dwarf—" Fall to and eat,

Ye good, ye evil !—as, by God's Rood,

God's rain cometh on evil and good !"

XII.

And now they know, that in God's name,

Had come this Dwarf to do them shame,

For shameful sin ; or honour bring,

On knight or dame who feel no sting

Of evil conscience, misshapen thing.

And none have fear to eat this food—

This Dwarf hath spoken " by God's Rood."

An hungered were they all to eat ;

But some eat, only palate to cheat.

And all did marvel much to see

Such as each craved, such food got he ;

And with true weight of silver and gold,

With cup and flagon, may not be told

How groaned the board.   But Quex gave groans

For sins that nevermore get loans.

XIII.

But said the king : " Faith of my life !—
As hath Sir Cradocke, our doughty knight,
I would that each had such a wife :
And ne should quail our court at sight,
Of uncarved Boar's Head and a Knife."

THE SILVER WEDDING.

PART II.

LIBRARY AND LARDER.

I.

THE day its frozen hours adown had rolled,
From rugged morn to melt on forenoon soft,
And slippery, and rutted deep with thawing mud :
The drip from eaves, from trees, from fences, told
The time, by water-clocks a thousand fold
Attesting, drop by drop, that long the scud
Of morning clouds had fled from sun aloft
Now gone to warm the earth ; and anon, anon,
And yet anon, a falling icicle, on
The porch step dash'd, with diamond clappers rang

G

The passing hour of noon, to forenoon verg'd ;
But not the shortening shadows far had verg'd
Toward the zenith, to fall from brink of noon ;
When Bran Cradocke his library enter'd and sang
Joyously : entering joyously : joyously the boon
Remembering on his Silver-Wedding morn,
Given his youth—a prayer and grant, in one
Good gift from God—the boon of a dear, good wife,
The wife of his youth, and thro' his lengthening life,
The credenced idol of his heart, alone
Enshrined there, and none other : and the worn,
Frayed heart-strings, fretted long by fitful time
In varying moods of joy, or grief, once more,
In playful reminiscence, stirred a tone
All resonant, with ardour, and the love-lore
And cheerily, hopefully sad and tender rhyme
Of a young man's song, exuberantly glad with fond
And longing, happy dismalness—a frond
Of song :—

CHANSON AMOUREUSE DE LA JEUNESSE.

I.

O queen, my homage bring I thee,
But dread thy royalty ;
Ah, deign to touch the hand thy slave
Holds up in loyalty ;

My life I crave,

O queen, from thee,

Ever thy slave :

O queen, my queen ! thy vassal save
Who dares thy royalty.

II.

My life !—there were for me no life,
No light, wert thou, not, darling, mine
For thee my heart and veins are rife
With bounding blood all thine

For thee this strife,

For thee I pine,

For thee I live :

G 2

My queen !—I pray, ah, bid me live,
And twine thy life with mine.

III.

No light !—thine eyes are all my light :
In shade my heart congeals,
My soul despair enshrouds with night,
When love its glance conceals.
Starlight-bright !
I'll kiss thine eyes,
I'll quaff their light,
O queen !—and heart and soul delight
Now love its glance reveals.

IV.

My love !—oh, sweetest, best, my love !
O dear control—but free
Thro' love and pardon !   Say this, **Love**,
This sweetest melody—

" I am thine, my Love,"

Ah, be thou mine,

My doubts remove,

Oh queen, my life, my light,—my Love !

My soul's whole melody !

                          —: this rote

Of love, Bran Cradocke sang : and singing smiled

With humorous self-irony, and satire mild

And kindly mocking, at the gushing note

Of youth, now thunder'd in the mighty bass

And deep-chested voice rolled out from massive

      throat,

Of portly *moyen age* advanced to pass

And ent'ring defile between the white-capp'd hills,

But strong and lusty yet as the hillside oak

Whose gnarled and knotty muscles, wrestling, broke

The storm-king's force—tho' now, decay the rills

Of life begin to choke, shall, long, his feet

Firm-planted still, dug thro' the slippery sleet,

Hold vantage ground upon the snow-capped hills,

Against the wintry blast.

II.

Thus hale and strong,

Bran Cradocke was.   And humorously the song,

Youth's ritornell' he sang ; for *moyen âge*

Deals flippantly with sentiment—knowing rage

Of passion sunk to calmer tides that fill

The holy life-harbours, with currents still

But eddying happily about the moorings cast

For anchorage safe and sure—the Doldrums past.

And through his house, resounding went that song,

Absorb'd, its youthful tenor, in the bass

Of lordly old-oak manhood : all along

The huge-chimney'd, antler'd, pictured, wainscot hall,

Echo'd that voice : from library to inner recess

Of household penetralia : even pass'd thro' wall

Of larder,—as knew the singer, and meant, it should—

Where sat his matron-wife, in conference deep

With comfortable housekeeper ; intent herself to keep

A watchful oversight ; of a truth she would

That naught might lack of hospitality,

Or shame housewifery, on this great day of state,

Her Silver-Wedding Day, that most should crown

Her finish'd wifehood with reality

Of honour well deserved : and so, the brown

Of roast ; of the done, or underdone,—relate

This, ah ! who can ?—or of done too much ; of just

The right proportion due of pound, or cup,

Or spoon ; or, of the much caution lest the crust

(Upper and under), right tint should fail to bake,

Or martyr'd be, with partial heat burnt up,

Or scorch'd, one side, too much : all this and more,

Did anxiously the matron wife enforce

On buxom housekeeper ; nor fail'd to charge

This last—"And Meadows *don't* forget the doves,

And teal with olives ?"—O trine auspicious !—" he loves

Them well—as do all gentlemen."   Thus the life,

The light, the queen and, first and last, the love

Of Bran's enamour'd song of youth (song now

Great-organ voice'd in hearty age) thought how

To compass skilful providence; and prove

Her housewife care for him should never cease;

Thro' very womanhood, impell'd to please

Her lord, as first: next all his sex.

III.

All these

These inner housewife mysteries, partly known,

Are rather guessed.   For who would dare the frown

Of queen, in larder throned?—ay me, not you,

Nor Bran the henpeck'd—Bran, the fearless, he,

But Bran (as all men are, or ought to be)

Good, and true, and brave, and henpeck'd, too,—

Nor he who tells the tale: tho' else, he never knew.

So comfort reign'd, as all might see,

Where each held right authority,

In Library he, in Larder she,

Within that peaceful home.

And right it is, that she, the roast

Should rule, who makes home's comfort most:

And right that he his bonds should boast,

Nor shall he seek to roam,

Whose wife, disgrace shall never earn,

In aught; where ne shall boar's head burn,

But done, be ever, to a turn:

And he may carve it ever

Where she, his own true wife,

Makes these her own endeavour,—

The Boar's Head and the Knife.

III.

TERAPHIM.

THE LEGEND.

III.

THE MAGIC MANTLE.

I.

Now sated are most, with this strange feast
Of fish, or fowl, or fatted beast,
Or sparkling wine, as each doth feel
Desire, or thirst.   Nor such a meal,
Had they now for long time, made;
And many, for thanks, a bead have said,
(May all, pray we, as this they read),
When to further test their meed,
The Dwarf his hand in coate did reach
And spake,—"There is other yet to teach."

II.

Then forth, from next his heart, he drew
A robe to their admiring view ;
A costly mantle, and bade them see
Its preciousness and great beautie.
Its value rare, beyond all price
Of rubies or gems that do entice
The longing eyes of dames : each fold,
A wave of loveliness untold ;
Bedight with charming grace, its shape
Might seem yet comelier, to drape
A fair and comlie form ; of bright
And richest samite, purest white
Its inner stuff, but outer wove
In deepest royal tint of love
To softest velvet, hearts-ease tinct,
In earnest that, must thus be link't,
With beautie, chastity ; all hid,
The inner samite, save where thrid

A pure white border round the verge

With silver sheen soon seen to merge,

All mixtilined with broidered gold,

In one deep hearts-ease-purple, rolled :

III.

Like as when, toward eventide,

The western sun is seen to hide

Behind a pall of purple cloud,

That floats alone from distant crowd

Of low banked vapours, in mellow light,

With silver edge blent, yellow-bright,

On royal purple.   Not of dawn

On glimmering limit far withdrawn

Hath God now made Himself a rose,

An awful rose,* for doubtful hope.

For since the dawn, the sun uprose

To answer the voice upon the slope,

With beams reverberant.   And long

---

* Tennyson.   " The Vision of Sin."

The day wends toward the evensong,
To sing *Magnificat* for sure
And living hope, voiced virgin-pure :
And God hath set in the evening sky
An heartsease royal with purple eye,
Most glorious, heavenward, of heavenly
     birth,
Most in beautie toward the earth.

IV.

Then bade the Dwarf them all to see
This mantle wondrous with beautie ;
Beauteous without and chaste within,
As virgin pure from taint of sin.
And bid them mark a single pearl,
Beyond the ransom of knight or earl,
A priceless pearl no realm might buy,
Was set in gold to clasp thereby.
How wins this pearl on all beholders,
Clasping mantle on fair shoulders !

v.

And said the Dwarf:—"God save thee,
  king,
And thy fair Guinever, the queen,—
I hither bring this beauteous thing,
And would the queen might try it on,
And other dames.   It may be won
By dame who can most comlie wear it:
But better come none other near it."

vi.

This Mantle, of such fashion rare,
To gain, now hopes each envious fair:
Most comelie, herself, would each bethought,
So grievous envie within each wrought;
And all draw round the Dwarf, in fear,
Lest hateful other the robe should wear—
All save Sir Cradocke's modest dame,
Who, fain to look, demurred thro' shame.

H

VII.

"But,"—said the Dwarf,—"this Mantle rare,
Though well shapen, to look on fair,
Hath one small fault, one curious trait—
It neither will, a moment, keep
Its colour, nor shape, in fold or plait,
Whether, who wears it, wake or sleep,
On ladie who hath done amiss.
But, surely, none be here, I wis,—
How say ye?—none such dame can be
Herein this goodlie companie?"

VIII.

Then all the knights begin to quake,
And be in fear for their ladies' sake:
Yet, if dismayed the ladies be,
None can tell from what they see.
But Guinever, the haught and proud,
Within the Mantle would enshroud
Her queenlie form; for, in her pride,
She thought to force the robe to hide

Her guilt; she seized this Mantle rare
And threw it over her shoulders bare.
Ay me, 'twere better had this queen
Not tried the Mantle on I ween!
Not now the sight wins on beholders
When the Mantle touched her shoulders.

IX.

From top to toe, the Mantle rent,
As if, by shears sharp cutting, shent;
One time too long, one while too short,
It wrinkled, in most unseemély sort
On Guinever's fair shoulders bare—
Now barer left than erst 'twas there;
Its colour turned, most strange this thing!
Now red, now green, then sable hue,
Which when he saw, thus quoth the king:—
"Beshrew me, I think thou be'st not true!"

X.

At which she threw the Mantle down,
And the king bespoke, with wrathful frown:—

"I had rather beneath the greenwood tree,

In deserts live, than here to be

The sport, base king, of thy groomes and thee"*—

And to her chamber flew in wrath:

She may not bide this ruthless scath.

.

XI.

Called, next, Sir Kaye, on his own dame:—

"Put on this Mantle, if not to blame;

But, if guilty, 'twere best thou fear it,

Bide where thou art, come not thou near it."

How laugh the knights, how titter the dames,

In mirth to see; as if in flames

The Mantle together shrivel and shrink!

The ladie cast the Mantle down;

Ay me, she too, with the queen must drink

Her bitter cup; now, must she slink

To her room away, with shame faced frown

---

* The old ballad as quoted in Mrs. Hall's "Queens before
the Conquest."

XII.

Vivien,—Ettarre,—the garment tried,

Better if they, as babes had died ;

The Mantle shrunk, as if in dread,

To a tassel and a thread.

Another ; and still another, tried ;

Better for all that all had died :

As each and other did thus essay,—

Alack, alack, and well-a-day !

The Mantle still ever said them nay :—

Till Arthur, lest the Table Round

And Court should all be proved unsound,

Cried out—" If *any* here there be,

Whose ladie shall be loyal found—

Sir Cradocke, Sir Cradocke, of the Battle Knights
    Three,

Sir Cradocke the strong-soul—thou art he ! "

XIII.

Sir Cradocke, then to his beauteous dame :—

" Our greystone tower is held in name

Of God and Sainctes and Holie Church ;
I fear no ill can thee besmirch—
Wear thou this Mantle, in God's name ! "

XIV.

And then his ladie, the Mantle, wore :
'Twas as worn, thus, for aye before,
When the Dwarf's eye shone, as velvet, soft
And heartsease tinct on silver.   And oft,
All marvelled that so long before
They failed to see this Mantle she wore ;
And how they long had ceased to see
Its wondrous grace and great beautie.

XV.

On her fair form, whom now it draped,
In decorous folds itself it shaped,
As any ladie could wish to see ;
Hung never Mantle so gracefullie,
Nor colour changed, nor long, nor short,
It robed her in most seemélie sort :

And all the beautie of her youth,

And all the beautie of her truth,

And all the beautie of her soul

That brought her, scathless, to this goal;

And all the beautie of her love,

In wedlock ordained in heaven above,

Uprose and blushed thro' form and face

As the Dwarf turned on her eye of grace ;

And she became, her faith now tried,

In beautie as of the glorified ;

Her eyes, with tint still deeper, shone

Harmonious with the Mantle's tone ;

Her smile gave back the pearl its light—

The precious pearl, so tender bright,

That clasped, on bosom pure as fair,

The wondrous Magic Mantle rare :

And thus arrayed,—O fair to see !

O more than fair, such great beautie ! —

In royal purple heartsease tinct

And gold-welt on lustre silverie,

As chastity, with beautie, linkt,
She stands—in halo softlie spread
As nimbus round her form and head.

XVI.

Oh well I ween, in his evening sky,
Sir Cradocke an heartsease shall descry ;
And sing *Magnificat* for evensong,
And pray to Mary mother mild,
And to fair Christ our Lord, her child ;
For God *hath* set in the evening sky
An heartsease royal with purple eye,
Most glorious, heavenward, of heavenlie birth,
Most in beautie towards the earth.

XVII.

But Guinever the queen hath reign—
Ay me, that such should ever reign !—
In Arthur's court ; and would outface
The Dwarf to lessen her disgrace.

From her chamber, balconied,

A window hung; whence might she heed

What passed in hall. And when she knew,

Therefrom, Sir Cradocke's dame proved true;

With cries of passionate envie, she,

Therefrom, made charge that, wrongfullie,

Sir Cradocke's dame hath the Mantle won,—

Though other none the robe may don.

To Sir Cradocke, then thus the king :—

" By nail in rood and wound in hand!

Thro' all the land the fame shall ring,

That truest queen, in all the land,

Is faithful and true, as beauteous, dame !—

She earns the Mantle, who earns no blame;

Let others wear, as earned, their shame! "

XVIII.

And then the Dwarf rebuked the queen,

Most unlovely, now, his mien;

With sin, and shame, and envious pride,

His eye grew bold, yet sought to hide.

He freely told King Arthur, there,

That, chastened, should be Guinever.

More sharply still, he said the same

When he rebuked this erring dame ;

And told her plainly that now must she

Her pride allay, more lowlie be :

Too bold her carriage, too bold her ways,

Too free her speech, too tight her stays,

Her dress as wanton as her dance,

Too fond of loose, gay dalliance ;

Too easy to look on sights not pure,

But cannot things holie long endure ;

Too eager to know things best unknown,

No dame may tamper with vice full-blown.

Public blazon, too fain to seek,

Both soft and hard her beauteous cheek ;

Abroad in search of constant pleasure,

This dame keeps not, in home, her treasure ;

In sooth, not she will darn a stocking,

And girds to see her cradle rocking—

" Beshrew me "—Arthur thus here joined,—

" Or fills it with issue baselie coined ! "

" Yea," quoth the Dwarf,—" not this, true queen—

The mightie queen of fireside home !

Discrowned, disrobed, by me she's seen,

Sackcloth-girt in the evening gloame."

XIX.

" But thou, O king,"—the Dwarf then said :

And Arthur bowed his kinglie head—

" Hard, art thou, on this dame thy wife ;

Look well, Lord Arthur, to thine own life ! "

THE SILVER WEDDING.

PART III.

TERAPHIM.—I.

I.

Bran, master of Graystead was : but Helen ruled

As mistress ——— *yes.*   In all authority

Objective, Bran supreme, rever'd ; but she,

His Helen, queen still reign'd, a sovran queen

In subjectivity supreme, as well.

Nay, unknown supremest Helen rul'd,

Thro' will obedient, pliant, flexible,

That ever had its way : as ever seen

This is, of proper womanhood reserv'd,

With woman's sacred fraud, to act as might,

(Of conscience void she) to her, seem right,

Or for the best: as Eve the mother.   *And know

Ye all—perplext, and scarce your wits preserved,

To learn from Thales, Berkeley, Hume, or Kant,

From Fichte, Hegel, Reid, Descartes, or Comte,

Or Stewart, Hamilton, Spencer, Mill (distraught

And doubt-rackt, all all themselves, to know), and

    naught

Enlightened—know ye all, blind lights as well,

Not exempted ye, who cannot tell

Or teach true animism, from being taught—

Aye, know ye all, this real, true critique

Of reason pure (*der reinen vernunft*), not weak

Faint glimmerings-out from shut, dark-lantern'd

    Ich

Or Ego, or Non-Ego, Alter-Ego, or *Ding an sich*,

But clear and steady, sunlight definition :—

Object-subject is—subject-object ; more,

Or less commixt ; transposed ; together blent

------

* In a humorous sense here.

Or fused—or divers ; different thro' rendition

Of much one and the same thing diff'ring, diff'rently—

Twice negatively, one another indifferently ;

And objective, with subjective, form the splent

That, object-subject or subject-object, binds

In relation adjectively.   Thus, the muse,

Thus clear-eyed Poesy, the spirit-wingèd,

Flies thro', or o'er, the labyrinth—the wring'd

And mazing labyrinth, intricate, all ring'd

With circling argument, where reason winds

Thro' blundering metaphysics :—straight the muse

Her flight directs on spirit-wings and finds,

At once, this central truth that, wide, diffuse,

Nay all diffuse thro' all create, this rule

And principle do make the state and being

Of all create of God : this, clearly seeing,

Beholding reverently,—that, principle

Of object-subject is but male-female

Condition'd with relation that the All

Doth build, in agency reactive, of male,

Female, create, creative, all to call

To life or being, inorganic all,

Or organic : as the Lord of all shall will.

Then, know ye now the truth the muse unfolds :

Know *sex* for object-subject : sex that moulds

And forms all entity, objectively,   -

Subjectively ; condition'd, respectively

Male and female, of God ; unique, diverse,

To build His work, in all His Universe.

II.

In all His Universe ?   Yea, all : the All,

From uncondition'd Chaos, stirr'd to life

Or being, out of waste unform'd, to thrall

Of *law ;* in widening waves of being mov'd

By the passing Spirit of God ; for ever moved,

In endless tides, thro' endless ocean : the All,

Condition'd with relation ; built thro' strife,

Yet consonance, of like-unlike or sex

Self-complemental ; built, and to for ever

Build, around creative will and thought

Of God: the All, resultant from reflex

Of like-unlike by law enthrall'd and brought

To birth,—create, creative, recurring ever:

The All, the common chord of harmony—

The whole foundation-chord of harmony,

Perfect throughout the pealing spheres to swell

The Maker's praise.   Thrice worthy, noble,

    holy,

Thrice holy, with angels and archangels, sung,

And with all the company of heaven sung,

And with voice of creation gone wrong, redeem'd,

    sung

The hymn of the Ages pealing the death-song of the

    lowly

The death-song, of the lowly uplift to the nations in

    glory,

In healing, victory—"*It is finished.*"   Sung,

From sphere to sphere, thro' sphere to sphere, the

    story

Resounding thro' the Ages, how the Son,

Grand God, the mighty King and Lord of Glory,

Was born of Woman, humbling himself, and on

Himself the form of a servant wore; of woman

Born, a servant made, th' All-Father's Will

To work; the All to save from the All's foeman

And curse,—from death and sin, and imperfection.

For the All-Father gave Him All, and still

Of given should none be lost; but thro' perfection,

And for perfection of His Work, He All

Should have, and keep for ever—ever.   Spent,

Thro' anguish of creation's groaning pent

Wholly in Him, and faint from loss thro' rent

And piercing; spent, all spent, with labour thrice

Of finishing than of creation, thrice

His rest; her God with Nature : then, from pall

Of clouds all black with death, from clouds all rent

By holy light, uprose, thro' o'ercast dawn

Flush'd to ruddy health from His healing wing,

The Sun of Righteousness.   To death no sting,

Nor victory, now, to grave.   Full drawn,

Full diapason now that pealing sing

The works of God, all working now with hope,

Of swelling anthem thro' myriad octaves scored,

In gamut infinite, beyond the scope

Of earth-dulled ear.   Creation chants, restored

With holier altars ; solemnly with cope,

As if of God's forgiveness, vested all

Her choristers ; and the Mighty One. implored

As Father, Prophet, Priest, and Lord of All,

Creator, Sanctifier, Saviour-King,

In Godhead Triunite, from second dawn

Of holy light, bows down attentive ear

In awful, silent majesty to hear,

Forever pleased to hear or see His Work.

Ministrant in prayer and praise, and work,

The swelling anthem, sweetly, grandly sing,

With crescent peal full diapson drawn,

Bearing His Cross :—

" Hosanna Sanctus Deus Sabaoth

Superillustrans claritate tuâ

Felices ignes horum Malahoth."*

O Christ ! not unto us the glory be,

But to Father and Holy Ghost with Thee

Triune,—to Thy Name Jehovah Malahoth !

O God Triune ! non nobis Domine.

All-Father ! Thy majestic Word,† Thy Thought

Reveal'd, commanding : and around Thy Thought

Thy Soul, Thy Holy Spirit, built and wrought

Thy Deed, the All : Thy Son, before all worlds

Begotten God of God, working with Thee,

Coequal wrought in the coequal Three—

O God, Thou Three in One !   From Chaos brought

Was then Thy Deed, the All, unique, concrete,

In causation secondary, in quest, eternal

Of mate to mate : Thy Power supernal

Us brought, Thy deed the All, by law and mete

Condition'd with relation, built thro' strife

---

* Dante (Paradise : Canto vii.—Cary). † Goethe's Faust.

Yet consonance of sex, in life-unlife,*

Self complimental; built with light and heat,

We build around creative will and thought

Of Thee. ELOHIM!—created we adore

Thy Power, beholding its magnificence,

ADONAI MALAHOTH; and Thee implore,

Wielder of the Two Realms† All-one in Thee,

And Thou in All! of Thy beneficence,

O SHADDAI! giver of each perfect gift,

To whom the hymns of thankfulness we lift,—

To bless Creation to perfection brought

Thro' Sacrifice of Thee, and ever wrought

In sacrifice, in loss and gain, from naught

Of void unform'd, to glory. Hail, to Thee!

All hail! Father Omnipotent, We praise Thee!

Immanuel! Prophet, Priest, King, We praise Thee!

O Soul of God, Light and Life-Giver, We praise Thee!

Thou Three in One! Thou One in All! We praise

    Thee!

---

* 1 Cor. ch. xv., v. 36.   † Spirit and matter.

TERAPHIM.—II.

I.

Lord, not only sendest thou the wind
To build in lofted heavens the organ clouds
That jar all earth and air with music stern,
And grand with volum'd thunder of thy voice
Ton'd in majesty, from domed darkness,
Window'd in sudden lightnings of thy glory :
Not only, Lord, the wind thou makest go
With breasting aid for dizzy flight, up where
The eagle, cloak'd with folded wings,* on crag
Stands close to the sun, and calmly gazes back
On sunward circlings no lesser wing could dare—

* In allusion to (reported) assertion of Mr. Tennyson that
he has written his last poem. In this connection, it may be
remarked, that it must be obvious why, in this tribute paid to
the genius of Tennyson, Coleridge, Longfellow, George Herbert,
and others, quotation marks are not used.

Song-Eagle ! laureate with loneliness :

Not only, Lord, thy breath in storm-blast came

Thro' ice, and mist, and snow, and turned did blow

The good south wind, where soon the white foam flew

Before the furrow following free, into

That silent sea wherein, nine fathoms deep,

Dream-hidden swims the plaguing sprite : not only

Eddying around the church porch, waits the wind

To waft to Thee a reverent, holy song

Of praise ; nor only whirls thro' fiend-sieg'd belfry

Whose bells, the open-throated swallowing bells,

Fresh inspirate, give forth in ghostly clangor

A Golden Legend ; nor thro' tree-tops only,

Bears the wind melodious streams of song.

From birds, high-perch'd, on branches sway'd

And dipping in the current stay'd, uprais'd,

Rippled by quivering leaves to rhythmic waving

Golden-green, in summer sunlight : aye,

And there be many birds swim on the wind,

To sing in joy for the smiling corn that bends

In mirth away, before their flight ; or, on

The fresh wind balmy with the breath of morning,

Comes, thro' the woodbined casement, song of birds,

The cheerful song of sweetly singing birds,

Throstling among sweet apple-blossoms of spring

To wake the sleeping homestead soon for bath

Of rosy light ; or thro' refulgent noon

The wind goes now, a tempering breeze, for birds

Whereon to float, and peck from luscious fruits

Their ripen'd richness turn'd toward sun, and sing

A full-fed song ; aye even, Lord, the wind,

Thou sendest calm'd to gentle evening air,

To bear quick-darting little humming-birds,

Their sweets to drain from honeysuckles train'd

To tempt with freshen'd leaves by evening showers

Fresh gemm'd, the western sun to stay his gaze

From porch, where smiling sit, in quiet talk,

The elder folk, or watch, in pleased musing,

Happy gambollings of happy children

Shouting the children's battle shout, joyful

With rose-peltings:—a distant, rumbling sound,

From out the gathering southwest—

Swiftly nearer, nearer, coming on,

Coming with a majesty of clouds

And great darkness, that hides the shaken earth

Smote to jewell'd smoke by bounding ice sparks

Shot myriad-showering, as if from mighty wheels

Cloud-envelop'd—the rushing, mighty wind,

O God!—the rushing, mighty wind! the breath

That goeth from thy nostrils out and makes

The morning stars to sing together, above

The cloud-capp'd towers!*—the rushing, mighty
    wind!

The breath that goeth from Thy nostrils forth

Among the spheres, unto the uttermost

Of suns that swoop thro' space with ponderous
    planets,

To bear from Thee, to Thee, the anthem-peal

Of Thy whole universe, this music scor'd

---

* Tempest.

Throughout the spheres, upon Eternity

And time ! nor lost a note, nor tone, nor sound,
    nor word,

Nor thought, nor rhythm.*   Nay, Lord of all, nay,

O God ! the cries, the shrieks, the groans of agony

The curses, blasphemies, red sounds† of battle

And blood, of rending for prey, or hate, or food,

None lost are these throughout the spheres !—these
    are

But discords, harsh and grating dissonance

Of loss and gain, of loss to gain, of strife

Thro' will left free, of somewhat right of choice—

The something left for choice, that men call
    chance—

Thy Works have, all, from Thee, to work Thy
    will :

---

* Alluding to the agreement between Sir W. Hamilton and
Mr. Babbage, that the battle of Actium might still be seen if
the sound and sight waves could be overtaken.

† Sounds have colour through instantaneous condensation.

And Thou the wrath of man makest to praise Thee :

Thou makest sin, and sorrow, and death to praise

    Thee :

In waste that is not loss, Thy Works all praise Thee :

These discords settest Thou, as notes all mark'd

With Thy Changed Cross for rest, in that grand

    score

Wherein Thy mighty hands, spanning the mighty

Diapason, grasp their dissonance

For lustre of harmonies prepared, resolved,

Compell'd by Thee, O Thou Great Master, to mix

And melt in harmony restored, eternal :—

The rushing, mighty Wind !

The wing'd chariot of the Lord and the horsemen

    thereof !

To bear up, heavenward, His chosen Inspired !

The rushing, mighty Wind !

And yet—

A still small voice :

The voice of desert air light-breath'd ; waking

The fire, in lonely musing left unwatch'd,

Unnoticed, to steal from lonely desert camp,

And creeping slow, low-crouching thro' dead grass,

To spring from its charred tracks with roars and
    glance

Of flame, upon the tall, dead prairie sedge,

And share its prey with the up-whirling Wind

That loads, upon the freighting clouds, dead ashes :

Only dead ashes ; but yet may spread a haze

Of dreamy Indian-Summer ; shaken dust,

From track of travelling clouds that pass

The Eagle's crag, and drop their fatness down

Upon broad lands enrich'd of yore :

A still, small voice—

The voice as of a lonely song ;

Of bird sad-plumaged, sitting lone ; on reed—

Only a shaken reed—but shaken, trembling ;

Bent before the rushing, mighty Wind

Thro' unkempt locks of tall swamp-cypresses

Blowing, and in their waving grey beards caught,

And check'd, to moan about their feet among

The rustling reeds, whence comes the humble voice

Of lonely bird : on only shaken reed

Bending before the mighty stream of hymning

Borne, from Thee to Thee, upon Thy breath

Outgoing forth thro' spheres, among the stars

That sing together above the cloud-capp'd towers

And rolling thunder of the organ-clouds.

II.

O rushing, mighty Wind and breath of God

That bears thro' time, and thro' Eternity,

This hymn of the Ages ! this whole grand anthem-
   peal,

This music mightiest in the mightiest,

From uttermost to uttermost, thro' sphere

To sphere, thro' sun and planet, thro' the Earth's

Four corners ; blowing on Chaldean tents,—

From Himalayas, back to Himalayas,

Circling ; over wastes and wilds ; o'er lands

With belfries spired, thro' lofty tree-tops chimes,

Of silver-mixt bell-tones, rolling ; to blend

With noble song from high-perch'd tuneful birds

Quiring with field and homestead songsters sweet,

And voices of laughing children : yet, to these—

Yea, Lord, not only sendest Thou Thy breath

Forth thro' the spheres,or buildest organ-clouds

About the towers, near eagles' eyrie, or

Inspirest tuneful songs of high-perch'd birds,

Or songs that cheer the homestead—aye, to these,

Not only : nay, my God, the Hymn of the Ages,

The song of the Lowly uplift to the nations in
    glory,

May the lowly hear and join : not only Thou

Thro' sacred madness of the bard makest

Music,* but, in being of the humblest,

Even Thy humblest, has Thou put a song ;

For full enharmony of Thy creation

Working Thy works, thro' quest of mate to mate—

---

* Tennyson : The Holy Grail.

Even lowest bacteria—even in parthenogenesis—
Self-complimental : the All, in prayer, praise, work,
All worshipping toward Thee !

III.

A new symphony, " Glory to God on High "—
Of men and angels singing praise to God,
Bursts out from Heaven and Earth : the symphony
Of Christmas this, as writ in Heaven's score :
First in Judæa heard ; where long time gone,
From Isräel's great harp King David smote
The songs of Zion's hope : bursts out in joy
The Christmas Symphony, from angel choir
Responsive rank'd of Che'rubim and Se'raphim,
     for ever ;
And men do chant it still to sound of shawm
And trumpet ; and of organ rolling surf
Of music billows surging mightily :
Bursts forth the Christmas Symphony :—
But first, a soft prelude, an angel sings,

The Annunciation, this :—" Hail Mary ! Hail

Thou full of grace ; and bless'd thou among

Women : Fear not, for with thee is the Lord ;

And thou, with God, hast favour found.   Behold,

The Holy Ghost shall come upon thee now ;

The Highest's power shall overshadow thee ;

That holy thing which shall be born of thee,

Parthenogenerant* thou of God's own Spirit,

Shall Son of God be call'd.   And, God of God,

Thus, He : Son of the Highest : Son of God,

Of God thus wedded to humanity

For full self-complement of His own glory,

Very God of God and Light of Light, yet God

Made man,—of His Kingdom shall there be no end."

And soon now,

Softly thro' th' expectant harmony,

And blending sweetness with Creation's hymn,

Glides in among the chords,

---

* Sesquipedalian,—but the only word that conveys the
shade of meaning.

A woman's voice—

The voice of a woman, in maternity

Exultant : singing a cantata, grave,

And sweet, and rising in rich-throated fullness,

From her innermost being, in very triumph

Of motherhood,—" My soul doth magnify

The Lord ; my spirit hath rejoice'd in God

My Saviour." This is writ " Magnificat "

Or song of Virgin Mother,—song of a mother

Virgin-pure, exultant that her womb

Shall bear a son who shall be great, a King,

And Saviour of men. Soon bursts forth now

The Christmas Symphony from Earth and Heaven :—

" Gloria in Excelsis Deo—In the Highest,

To God be glory, and on Earth be peace,

Good will toward man." The Symphony, this is,

That sings the hope of the longing All, fulfill'd

In the hymn of the Ages, the deathsong of the Lowly

Uplift to the nations in glory.

IV.

And all may hear

And sing, as shall be given of voice and ear,

The all-harmony: in part, each only ; even

As every fiery prophet could but speak

His music by the framework and the chord : *

And some hear only dissonance, and sing

True notes in false accord ; even such false tones

As viols, perfect else and priceless, may

At last give out, when too long resonant

With false vibration thrill'd from others near.

Thus false of ear and voice are they that sing

" Lo, here is Christ,—or Christ is there : "—or sing

" My brother, I that harp to thee, lo ! I am Christ ;

And thou, too, brother, listening, art with me,

A Christ: each in our joint humanity."

Ay, me, my brother, that those notes, those sweet

True tones, in false vibration caught and mangled,

---

* Tennyson.—" The Holy Grail."

K 2

Should sound distuned from harps of jangling
    strings.

    Thou art Christ, as thou art join'd with Him,
And He in thee, as one with thee : but not
The Christ art thou—lo, brother ! hear the Pæan
Of triumph—this last peal, that shakes and rounds
With fullness all the swelling harmony :—

    " Christ is risen !

      He is risen indeed !

      And hath captivity led captive ;

      For as all die in Adam, even so

      In Christ shall all be made alive ! "

O brother, even sweet spring flowers burst
The grave of dark, cold winter, and sing
To you the Easter Anthem—upward look,
From introspect diseased, of thine own self,
Out from thine own self, turn thy gaze above,
And let thy vision pierce a whirling void
Thro' clouds and thro' the brooding darkness

Brother !—lo *there*, is Christ !—lo, there on High !

Enthroned in glory of the Father—*there!*—

All clad upon with thy humanity,

With thy humanity above thee raised,

That thou mayest struggle up above thyself,

God helping thee, from God to God in man ;

And with the Father and the Comforter,—

Aye, will he come and dwell with thee ; and thou

Shalt be at one with God ; but brother, thou

Art not the Christ.   The Christ is God, who

Born of a virgin was : and died for us

On Calvary : and rose again, the God, the man,

To God's right hand.   And he shall come again,

Shall judge the All, entune disharmony,

Shall wipe all weeping eyes : the Lord of Lords,

The Christ, the Lord himself, the mighty Lord !

Shall bow the heavens down and come to judge

And punish : and the dead shall rise again

Before the Christ : and there shall be, of sins,

Forgiveness : and the Everlasting Life.

v.

Toward that great day, flows ever on, the stream

Of boundless harmony, from God, thro' all

His work, rhythming back to God new chords

Of being called to life : from God to God,

Thro' endless ocean moved to rhythmic waves,

To stormy grandeur lash'd by passing breath

Of His Spirit, rolls, in endless tides, the stream

Of mating harmony ; and they therein

That dwell, that great Leviathan, or least

Infusory, do all praise Him : and earth,

Built of their loves that die to live again,

Builds ever harmonies anew, thro' quest

Of mate to mate.   For what the mystery

Of generation, aye, of creation what

But passing on of God's own Spirit through

The All ; out of crude, void, unform'd, to form ;

Thro' object-subject, male-female, create

Creative through relation, that the All

Doth build through sex reactive ; all to call

To life, or being, inorganic, all,

Or organic : as the Lord of All shall will.

VI.

For ever, ceaseless, roll the rhythmic waves

Of harmony, from all His Work to God .

For ever pleased to hear and see His works,

Creation's Anthem sweetly, grandly, sing,

With crescent peal full diapason drawn,

Bearing His Cross.   And they of earth best hear,

As given is to earth-dull'd ear to hear,

Who stand where ebbs and flows in endless tides,

And strands drift-tokens of the far unknown,

This endless ocean of being and praise,

About the mount of God.   Aye, there it is

As if God, pleased to hear and see His works

Ministrant in prayer and praise and work

Throughout the All, Himself, in human voice,

Deign'd with gentle accompaniment to join

Creation's song, in octave full of blessing

Key-noted with humility, all based

On purity: for that, the lowly, hope

Should have, thro' the Lowly uplift to the nations in
      glory

And the pure, the pure in heart—they should see
      God.

VII.

Yes there: there where the spheral harmony

Enrounds the Earth, and ebbs and flows in rhythm

Among Judæa's hills and vales, upon

The Mount of God, and meets sweet rills of mercy

Flowing past the Hill of Sacrifice,—

There in Jewry known, best known, is God:

And there best heard, the harmony of God

In all His Work ; and as if heard in song

Low-voicèd—" By the Brook Cedron "—of a mother,

Soothing child to sleep when crickets chirp

On hearth, from mate to mate ; when evening air,

Drowsy with the summer breath of flowers,

Floats the all pervading hum of life

Thro' window ; or when with thunder the heavens

Burst, and lightenings flash in on the child

Safe in the mother's arms, and calm'd in awe

That God our Father speaks from Heaven out,

As He from Sinai spoke, and is the great

I Am, the God in All, and over All.

And other songs of Zion,—Lord ! blessèd she that

   sings

The songs of Zion to her child ! and he,

In dreams of night, in the night of his age,

Shall hear them still,—songs all of Zion's King ;

Of God made man, and of a virgin born,

A babe in manger laid, and by Three Kings

Of Orient homagèd as the Christ : and songs,—

What time his mother sought Him sorrowing,

And once stood, in great dolor, near the cross

On which He died that all might live through Him

At one n harmony with God : and songs,—

Of how a halo shone about His head,

And beautiful His feet, on golden light

Shadow'd, as on Judæa's hills He walk'd,

Good Shepherd seeking sheep estray'd :

And other songs,—of how Christ bore the griefs,

The pains and sorrows of humanity ;

And sooth'd them, healing sick humanity ;

And bless'd the family, in that he made

The Marriage Wine a miracle of power

Of Him who made from the beginning, them,

Who should from all else cleave together twain

In one, male and female,—Himself begot,

The Seed of the Woman, of humanity,

His highest, wedded to God, for blessing

Of His lowest building all through quest

Of mate to mate : and bless'd the family

In that, should be destroy'd degraded types

That Terah pattern'd first, for household gods,

From the Ark of Safety, types soon begrimed

With bloody superstition :—and false gods,

And fear of Moloch, should from the hearth be
 driven.

VIII.

The All builds all thro' quest of mate to mate,

One God is all in all, in least. in great ;

And God made Man, who bless'd the Marriage Wine,

Creator, Sanctifier, Saviour, trine,

The God, of Cherubim on high adored and Seraphim,

These Three in One are yet the household Teraphim.

And These—

Aye, These ! the Teraphim in that grey stone
 steading ;

Where the sun went down, and out from heaven were
 hung

The silver starlights, on the Silver-Wedding

Of faithful pair, who all through life had clung,

God-join'd, with truthful love that naught had riven,

Nor man, nor clash of will, nor disasters leaven.

And there was worn,

Unsoil'd, untorn,

As pure as pure could be,

Nor wrinkl'd, nor shameless shrunk, nor stretch'd too
long,

Nor colour changed, nor task'd to hide a wrong,—

The mantle of Chastity.

————————

IV.

IN MEMORIAM.

THE LEGEND.

IV.

THE GOLD-WROUGHT HORN.

I.

" ANOTHER gift would I bestow "—
The Dwarf said, (Oh ! that he would go,
This horrid Dwarf ! from hence away,
Nor ever hither come !—now pray
The dames)—" one other gift would show
To King and all the Table Round :
But, first, 'tis meet that all should know
This gift may prove some knight unsound."
So fain to have the Dwarf away,
The dames would bid him, now, to stay.

II.

Then from the scrip hung at his side,
Much soiled with mire, winestained, worn,
And, like a palmer's, long and wide,
The Dwarf drew forth a drinking horn :
Nor ever was horn more richlie wrought,
Than this the Dwarf in scrip had brought.
He showed it held on golden legs,
Carved as brawny lion's paws ;
Of diamant, the drinking pegs
Mark on gold, down to the dregs,
The lawful stint of temperate laws ;
And round the brim, a crown of gold,
The rich red wine, in bound, might hold.

III.

And quoth the Dwarf—"Now know ye all,
None other this so richlie wrought—

None other this than very horn

From head of ox that knelt in stall,

When Christ our Lord a babe was born ;

By Joseph of Arimathea brought

To Glastonbury from Palestine,

With holy cup that held the wine,

The sangreal of Christ.   His weal

Was, under Vespasian's hand and seal,

Commended to the Britons' king,

The king Arviragus, whom Rome

Held tributary.   And so the king

Was gracious ; and bestowed a home

At Glastonbury, twelve hides of land,—

One hide to each,—on Joseph's band

Of freres, when Joseph was sent forth

By Philip the Apostle, to light the north,

That thro' the fog of heathenesse

Might men our Lord's fair face confesse."

IV.

This Gold-wrought Horn he filled with wine,
Not Quex's, as sooth, may one divine ;
But with wine himself had brought,
Filled now, the Dwarf, this horn gold-wrought ;
And spake these words with manner dry :—
" He, who would win this horn, may try ;
And win it may he, easilie ;
Who, knight as dame, aye, he as she,
Is chaste and true ; nor fails ere now,
The knight to keep the knightlie vow,
And vigil true of temperance,
Besides devoir with sword and lance.

V.

" But knight may not of this horn drink,
'Twere better should he from it shrink,
Who spills three drops, but only three ;
For both are false, his dame as he :

He may not drink, but must refrain.

Who spills two drops, but only two,

Breaks only his vigil, but his dame's not true ;

Nor can this knight this gold horn drain.

Who only one drop spills, may win :

Tho' failed in vigil, yet true his dame ;

And he hath overcome his sin.

But only knight, from sin and shame

All free, may drink, nor spill a drop,

To win this horn.   No longer stop

To gaze "—said the Dwarf—" but fearless try :

Doubtless ye thirst—my speech is dry."

VI.

What ails the knights, that they gaze on still?

It seems that drink, none can, or will,

Where all are fain to drink their fill :

What ails the knights that not one stirs,

Yet all in battle have won their spurs ?

Wherefore passeth from dame to dame
Look triumphant, drowned in shame ?
Ay me ! doth each knight fear to spill
The wine, though fain to drink his fill !

•

VII.

The Dwarf then at the king looked hard,
And said :—" Sir Arthur !—laureate bard,
Than Taliesin greater, of thee shall sing.
In sweeter than sweet key of Gwynedd,
As aye true knight and ' blameless king ';*
Likewise, thy judges, in law much read,
Do say the king can do no wrong :
So honour we both, the law, the song ;
Nor offer thee I this horn to win :
A king should be blameless of shame and sin.
But hard wert thou on the queen thy wife ;
Look well, Lord Arthur, on thine own life."

---

* Tayles of the King.—Tennyson.

VIII.

· And as on him the Dwarf did gaze,
With eye wide open, yet filmed with haze,
The king became as one asleep,
Yet searching with sense of unknown loss,
Who nears a brink of bog ooze, deep,
And hidden under treacherous moss ;
Alone, with eyes stared in the daze
Of false witch-fires, beyond, ablaze :
And he had fallen : but the Dwarf's eye
Grew red, as with the blushing light
That wakes the day, and from the sky
Drives veiling darkness of the night :
And then the king recovered sight,
And caught himself, and stood upright.

IX.

And now the court do call to mind
How the king had seemed to find

Something gone from out his life,
Unknown to him how false his wife ;
Something missed, that made him seek
Restless joyaunce ; made him weak ;
Made him prey to wanton eye :
And well-nigh fallen was he thereby.
But when the king now stood upright,
As the Dwarf's eye blushed with rosy light,
All know the bard, for aye, may sing,
Of him, true knight and ' blameless king.'

x.

Then, one by one the horn they try,
None can this urgent Dwarf deny ;
And many an one, the drinking horn
Makes fain to wish him never born.
As each one tries, the Dwarf his scrip
Holds under the horn, to catch the drip :
Ay me, for scrip with wine soon soaked—
Ay me, for knight whom wine hath choked !

Some fancie themselves to drown with wine ;

Some, never but water to drink, incline ;

The scrip grows, more and more, winestained ;

But the Gold-wrought horn, no knight hath
  drained.

Quoth Dwarf,—" Of all the Table Round,

Can never a knight who drinks be found ! "

XI.

Then, to Sir Cradocke, his ladye said :—

" Dear lord, thou truly mayest not dread

To win this Gold-wrought drinking-horn :

My truth on it ! tho' all may fail,

This thou shalt win for me this horn ;

Thy strength shall now prove thine avail."

" Yea : "—quoth the king—" fair dame, well said !

For thy good lord, thou need'st not dread."

Wherefore aloof, doth Sir Cradocke stand ?—

Nor toward the horn reach forth his hand !

XII.

Whereon, the Dwarf on the knight bends eye
None may this awful Dwarf deny.
Sir Cradocke then his hand reached forth ;
Now shall be known how true his worth.
And as the Gold-wrought horn he took,
From head to foot he trembling, shook,
As fire of battle from the Dwarf's eye shot ;
And the knight became as one who, hot
With struggling, a wrestling victorie sought.
His thews did strain and gnarl and knot ;
It was as tho' his soul now wrought
In tears, with agony of strife :
" Not e'en knew I "—thought the dame his wife :
And when he raised the Gold-wrought horn,
He trembled as ne'er since he was born ;
'Twas only trembling of hard strained strength
Still quivering from the battle's length :

Yet he one drop of wine hath spilled,
One only drop of all that filled
The Gold-wrought horn.

XIII.

Now know they all,
God's wounds had bled afresh for him
Tho' doughty knight, who still might fall :
And all now know the gold crowned brim
May safely hold the wine within ;
Lost only this one drop, of all.
And thus the knight this horn did win,
For he had overcome his sin,
With truer vigil of temperance,
Besides devoir with sword and lance.

XIV.

As fire-purged silver, clear and bright,
The Dwarf's eye shone. Assoiled of wrong,

Sir Cradocke the Strong-Arm'd, the Battle Knight,
The knight with soul, as arm, so strong,
Did then, before that courtlie throng,
A reverence make to his beauteous dame,
His beauteous dame of fairest fame :
And said, holding the Gold-wrought Horn
To her who hath the Mantle worn :—

XV.

" My ladie dear, mine own true wife !—
'Tis the day of days in all my life :
Five-and-twenty years are past,
Since thou became my first, my last ;
But only the years have stored away
Their dates—'tis still our wedding day,
This day on which this evening sun
Is profit of another won
To set in gold.   But now I spy,
As wrought with silver, in our evening sky,

A royal heartsease of great beautie,

Upon the golden heaven beyond,

In token of sweet love and dutie

That us have linkt in heaven-made bond.

In memorie whereof, I drink to thee ;

Drink thou, too, dear dame, with me,

Of this, the wine the Dwarf hath brought,—

Thy lips best crown this Horn Gold-wrought ! "

XVI.

Then drank the knight from the gold-crowned
    brim

And, making reverence, then pledged she him.

Not other drop, of all that filled

The Gold-wrought Horn, again, was spilled ;

Nor held it dregs, through magic laws,

This horn with gold-carved lion's paws :

And passed, between this God-joined pair

Of doughtie knight and ladie fair,

The looks of love from heaven lent
To marriage, made in heaven above.
Of twain in one together blent:
God-joined they—for God is love.

XVII.

Now all the court and Table Round
Do make the hall's carved roof resound
With loud acclaim; all under sway
Of that dread eye they must obey,
Tho' envie hold that goodlie array.
And cried the king,—" Thou truest knight,
By God his wound that bled anew,
For thee!—oh! may this saving sight
Of us, and all, as thee, be true!—
Still further honour will we show;
That, to all time, our realm may know
True knight, and ladie true as fair,
In wedlock true, as God-joined pair.

Fill goblets,—not such,"—so spoke the king,—

As dwarf may melt, but dwarf doth bring ;

And fill with wine the Dwarf hath brought,

Wherefrom was filled the Horn Gold-wrought.

XVIII.

" Now,"—said the king when all had filled ;

And the Dwarf's eye gave, thereto, assent—

" Fear not we, that wine be spilled

So consecrate with true intent.

From royal hall, here in Caergwent,

We do for ever and aye ordain,

In honour of this noble pair,

This use and custom to obtain

Throughout our realm, in hall or steading,

In town, or hamlet, of the Silver Wedding ;

Kept aye as marriage Jubilee

For faithful pair that joined be

Thro' five-and-twenty married years,—

Years, silver-plumaged, bedrent with tears,

Or swift with joy.   Of silver, all,
Shall be the tokens, in cot or hall ;
Be token great, or be it small."

XIX.

" And drink we now "—said on the king—
" To health of this true, noble pair ;
And wealth, and honours, may time long bring
Sir Cradocke and his ladie fair ! "
And then, in honour of these twain,
They all did drink.   And then, again,
With loud acclaim, did hall resound :—
May all, elsewhere, to join, be found !

THE SILVER WEDDING.

PART IV.

IN MEMORIAM.

I.

HELEN heard that youthful song of love
Which Bran, from mediæval chest of lungs,
Strong-ribbèd, roll'd cheerily thro' echoing hall,
From library to the larder.   And Meadows,
Seeing from her mistress' blush how fast
The years were rolling back before the car
Of youth's sun-god, grew smiling-bold to say
(For womankind from womankind claims part
And share in triumph) that naught, should library
Find amiss, that day, from larder: and,
Leaving there her mistress with the past,
Herself went forth to marshal victory.

II.

But Helen's soul went back to meet the god
Of youth's bright morn: went, soul with soul, with
     him
Who, heart and heart, with her, long years agone,
Had greeted Love's first coming.   For the song
Of Bran, sung now, was as a herald's voice
Proclaiming larger realm for Love; and as
The god came on, the years, off'ring tribute
Of memories, closed in behind his car,
A joyous, weeping, struggling, smiling train.

III.

And Helen felt how great Bran's love for her,
In all those years: knew all her love for him;
Knew how she had been helpmate true, to him;
And thought how little hands had held to him
Sweet pledges of her love and true wifehood:

And all the glowing beauty of her youth ;

And all the peerless beauty of her truth

And love, thro' all those passing married years ;

And all the holy beauty of her faith,

Of soul and life, well tried,—uprose and show'd

There all the maiden, wife and mother blent

In blushing beauty of crown'd womanhood.

And Helen rose and to her nursery went,

And saw her cradle empty nest, of young

No longer fledgelings ; and then from drawers

Took little socks, and kiss'd the little curls

Reap'd in tears from little heads now wing'd

As cherubim : and thence to her own room

Passing, she knelt at that bed undefiled,

Knelt where her maidenhood, to motherhood

Blooming, had died to give her cherubs birth.

IV.

Nor, in his library, writing, was Bran Cradocke

Less busy, *in memoriam* of what

M

Of joys, of care, and grief, of life, or death,

His five-and-twenty married years had hid

Away from sight of all save memory's ken—

The years that ring the marriage bells for birth,

And toll the knell of death.   And as he thought

On all those years, his countenance, at times,

Was moved as if by happiness, to smiles ;

Or broaden'd, with quaint, quiet humour, spread ;

Or anon, it wrought as if his soul with stress

Of feeling struggled, and manhood's tears fell

As wasteway waters dammed for husky grist.

And while he thought back on his wedded life,

The years became as into one year roll'd

That brought to him the bride of youth, and she

Became one bride—his Silver-Wedding bride

Of this his Silver-Wedding Day.   And there,

So rapt from time and place was he, that naught

He heeded of the gentle book-spirits

That round him wheel in silent guardianship.

Nor even heard he low and cautious laugh

That seem'd to test safe entrance thus,

Thro' door push'd cautiously ajar, for two

Who softly whisper'd " Father ! "   For his hands,

The father's own hands, tamper'd with by heart,

Had often turn'd traitors, to let in, thro'

Library walls impregnable else, these

Dear foes to quiet.   There, at door, stood now,

Red-hooded, with sash-wrapp'd cap, and shod with
     snow,

Two—boy and girl—well grown, but children yet,

With still unspent their wealth of childhood's fancy;

For they had come with glee to show their sire

What rich brown pipes, as meerschaums colour'd all,

Had this year's chestnut leaf-stems made.   But these

Even, the father heeded not.   And they,

Each to the other, look'd,—" Wherefore so mov'd,

Our father "—and awed, on tiptoe walk'd away,

Seeing that their father took no heed.

V.

For all the past loom'd up before Bran Cradocke :

As loom the Alps thro' clouds that feed with snow

The frozen river slowly moving down

In icy mass with grinding flow that rifts,

And ranges in long drawn moraines, the spoils

From mountain slope whereon, who stands, midway,

May feel the shock of chasms, and hear the voice

Of life from far-down, smiling valley fed

To verdure by the rills the frozen river

Melts to give.   Yet who there midway stands,

For panting rest with alpenstock, shall know

That still—above the valley and the clouds,

And Alps with frozen river ever melting,

For-ever bearing back to earth what was

From earth upraised—spreads over mountain top,

Heavenward, that serene, clear, purest ether

Deepening toward Eternity and God.

VI.

And as Bran wrote, it could not fail but that
The retrospect should sometimes blur with tears
The view of five-and-twenty married years.
For children had been born to them, and some
Were dead: and one was gone from out their gates;
And he, tho' living, had become as one
Dead to them, whose name was never named—
So grievous the naming of it—save in prayer.
Thus doom of trouble, born with man as upward
Fly the sparks, had not passed by the home
Of Bran and Helen ; and disaster's leaven
Struck their substance with consuming stroke
So fell, that hungry want bark'd at their door.
And sickness on the strong man came and beat
Him down, and cast him weaken'd to the sea,
Where scarcely could he buffet with the waves,
So great his weakness ; and well nigh the waters
Had gone over him : and blinded so was he

With bitter brine, that scarcely could he see,
Had nearly fail'd to say, " Save Lord, I perish ! "
But fail'd not : and help came : but if denied,
Still knew the strong soul of the man who now
In ivied greystone house sits grateful there
For house, and barn, and store, and blessings all,—
That in His Father's house were many mansions :
Yet had he well nigh sunk for very faintness.

VII.

But the woman was true woman, bearing griefs,
His griefs with hers : and was true wife, nor fail'd
To comfort ; nor the weakness of the man
Reproach'd, but help'd him, being true helpmate
To him ; and the hand she gave him, on this day
Five-and-twenty years ago, the hand
Slender and white and vein'd with Norman blood,
Did menial service ; but it was as hand
Of priestess sacrificing ; and often,
With humour seeking to hide the pathos of it,

Would he call her their inspired priestess,
And her kitchen a temple all glorious
With sacrifice and the oracles of fate.

VIII.

All this, and more, passed thro' Bran Cradocke's
    mind,
As if in stream that flowed where, on the bank,
Stood Recollection gathering drift from flood
And eddy—where waters, drain'd from hill and dale,
Had pass'd thro' varying scenes of rugged rock,
Or opening sun-lit valley, and swell'd to power
And depth, thro' rich, broad fields, past haunts of
    men :
But that from river headland chiefly seen
Is beauty of the landscape, and the river
Bearing, on its middle current, trees—
Some dead, dry trunks, and some, uptorn from roots,
Swept living, down the stream ; and sunken things
Thrown up by boiling eddies.

IX.

                    Thus, tho' Bran
Sat writing till the frozen waterclocks
Had ceased to tick, much more throughout the past
Had memory spread, than he could now record
Before the evening sun sent beams to hang
From mullion'd windows, of Graystead ivy-clad,
The glinting shields of golden light, on this
His Silver-Wedding Day.   But most he thought
On her, his Helen, his Silver-Wedding bride:
And thus of her he thought, and thus to her
He wrote :—

In Memoriam.

"A Good Wife is of the Lord."

———

Our Silver-Wedding Day !—
Our Silver-Wedding Day, O dearest Wife,
Bears royal rule o'er those that mark our life

With daily score of time. To day, we see

Our Wedding Day proclaim'd in Jubilee :

The date, not day, is changed.

O day of days !

That brought to me the Lord's " Good Gift " which
sways

Man's heart of hearts with wealth of treasure trove

On Earth, but found thro' compact made above

And full-possess'd by him, is seen so gemm'd

With joy complete, and crown'd with charms, that,
hemm'd

In circle of her faithful arms, her breasts

Shall satisfy his longing, and make rests

Whereon his heart may safely place its trust,

Close where its treasure is—a heaven where rust

Shall not corrupt its sheen : nor, need of spoil

Shall he have thus ; and, shunning all lewd coil

With else, shall keep him only unto her,

In miser's fear of loss lest death sever.

O day of days ! my soul, thro' years, in pride

And love, recalls the vision of my bride—

Bright vision of her I loved, and still do love,

Shall love, for ever, thro' each streek'd remove

Of Time dissolving to Eternity.

Bright Vision !—bright with light of beauty's might

That aches my gaze with straining and delight,

Beholding my belovéd one : with eyes

Half drown'd, too, in the stream whose rise

Took breadth from loveliness, and flooded all

My being with desire that shall not pall

With full fruition of the pure embrace :

For she was mine, and mine alone, thro' grace

Of Holy Church's blessing laid in laud

Of chastity, upon our hands, by God

In wedlock clinch'd thro' reverend priest, to weld

Such juncture of our wedded lives, that held

In oneness (thus the priest did speak the will

Of God, to all the company, lest ill

Should follow ignorance) no man might foin

With sunderance what God should thus conjoin.

Bright Vision! she who then stood by my side

In veiléd shrine for me alone, my bride

With orange blossoms crown'd, thro' all the years

Time freights with what of good or ill it bears,

Still turns to me those eyes with heartsease tint,

In earnest of the love that us had linkt,

And gemm'd with fluxure of the ruby fused

In garnet, for my worship. And the thrill

Of those dear lips in wedded kiss doth still

Record the loving promise of her heart,

To beat for me alone, until death us part.

  O day of days! my soul, thro' all these years

Pinion'd in winged flight with joys and tears,

Hath loved her for the worth which virtue tries

Against the weight of gems, and finds its price

Beyond what rubies can the scales disturb

In balance, with preponderance. No curb

Of doubt, thou day of days! doth fret the tread

Of Memory's train, by thee, in harness led:

But Honour guides the course, whereon do throng
Her pursuivants to herald all along
The route, and rich purveyance freely make
Of heartroom, and of love, for her dear sake
Whose car-borne image Memory thus convoys
To me, as far beyond all else in life
Most precious—O Image of my darling wife!
And mother of my children.   For she teem'd
With offspring, of our love begot; and seem'd
Far dearer when she gave to them, from me,
Their lives conceiv'd and nourish'd of her body.
God's Spirit breath'd them into life; but soon
Recall'd some: that so, might we, in loss,
Direct our gaze above the bloodstain'd Cross
To seek them near the Crown, with cherubs quir'd,
Awaiting us to join their song.   Untired,
They with restful service alway chant
God's praises; and with prayers re-chant
Christ's Intercession for their father, and
The mother who in pain did bear them, and

For sister, brother, all.   With us, are yet

Two left—O God! so grant our sun to set,

That we may see them bless'd of Thee,

As thou seëst best,—my only prayer this be

For them :—for *him*—no longer let him roam

Astray—be Thou Good Shepherd, Lord,—bring home

Our Son!

  O day of days ! I well recall

Her household labor deftly done in all

These married years : and all her early toil

While yet the sun wakes morning to uncoil,

With scanty light, the length of day ; that thus

She may give meat to all who in her house

Do dwell—with portion for her maiden too—

And clothe her household all with scarlet hue

Of Industry ; *her*, strength and honour clothe :

Her children, rising, call her blessed ; sloth

Doth not her steps delay—in truth, she lends

Too little thought to her own good, and spends,

For us, her life ; her husband praiseth her

In all that else she does, and is ; and hear

This : "let her own works praise her in the gates"—

Where (being fifty three—these awkwards dates !)

Her husband sits among the elders grave,

To sing,—in manner of Anacreon

(Himself a Presbyterian) which may don

A mood of lighter weft than suits the verse

That now belauds my wife—to rehearse,

I say, in alter'd strain of song, an ode

Of how, with creature comforts, our abode

She graced with pleasing skill ; and strove

In conflict dire against the demon stove

That gaped, with horrid, red-hot, flaming mouth,

Upon her and gave off (as in a drouth

The earth sends vapour to the sun) great cloud

Of greasy fumes in agony, with loud

But strangling bellow up the cavern-length

Of chimney, when it felt th' unsparing strength

Which raked its fiery jaws with poker, thrust

As lance full into them—O fearful joust !—

In grasp of slender, steel-strung hand with which

She eke the demon throttled with damper's twitch,

And tamed its heated rage to bear the ache

Of batter cold, poured on its scales to bake

For breakfast.   But, let now the theme be sung

On lyre, with Teian-Sapphic chords, well strung :—

CHANSON AMOUREUSE DU MOYEN AGE.

" Blest as the immortal gods " * was he

Who ate those buckwheats bak'd by thee !—

Fondly ate—and ate—and ate—

Nor feared the chill of frigid plate,

With long delay refill'd, should steal

Their warm life, and congeal

                    The butter's golden flow.

The table stood the stove so near,

In kitchen corner, that my dear

---

* Ambrose Phillips.—Sappho.

(Victorious o'er the demon black,

In struggle fierce, and with much thwack

Of raking poker), could transfer

The deftly lifted cakes, by her,

    " Neat-handed " to our plates.

Against the window raged the blast

With which the Windsbraut, all aghast

At its own sleety, freezing cold,

Howled for entrance to that fold

Of comfort, jealous of the care

Bestow'd by thee upon us there—

    Our household priestess thou !

But all in vain, it howl'd in rage

Of disappointment unassuage ;

And storm'd, in fury, off in flight

Around the corners—at the sight

Of buckwheat cakes fresh-baked by thee

For Father, Bran, and Na-ta-wee,—

    And dash'd th' icicles down.

But not alone do buckwheat cakes

Inspire to sing what for our sakes

My Love hath done.   Nor, poker-lance,

The only brand she wields : *large rents*

Attest her needle armed with thread ;

And who ?—ah, *who !*—can sing the bread

     The Nine could never make !

I'd rather eat it.   Only she

From spell may let the yeast-elf free,

And " set the sponge " to rise :—

As a fair bosom heaves with sighs,

And longs, in love's hot breath to dree,

A willing holocaust—ay, me,

     See the Muses' cake all dough !

This ne'er befell my Love's loaf-bread—

Let only Muses feel a dread

Of dough !   For if not one could bake

Among the Nine, how shall they take

         N

The measures fit for bread and rhyme ?—
Or temper oven's heat, in time
          To " soak " the sponge aright ?

But only she the sponge can " set "
To heave its bosom : or brunette
The tender crust make oven bake,
All tinted in so rich a lake
Upon its rounding breast, as can
The southern sun with beauty tan
          Fair maiden's blood-flusht cheek.

The secret of this magic bread
I must conceal.   One only thread
Of mystery unravelled may,
As book-mark, lie within this lay
And hint, what further search may show,
The Woman-heart, in weal or woe,
          Beseeks affection's help.

This knowledge found I at the end

Of mystic runes home-lore did lend

My Love for making bread; and which

She sang—lo! sparkling eyes!—a witch!—a

    witch!—

Whose sleeve-bare are flushed with hue

The flour would steal to blush in rue

        And envy of their fairness!

A Woman's speech, or written words,

Are alway postscript in the chords,

With Woman's meaning, most vibrate:

Nor failed my love to show this trait;

Most womanly of women, she

Ended thus the recipe:—

        " You *then*, Sir,—*kiss the cook!*"

" Kissing the cook " brings back pentameter:

A graver matter 'tis should Hagar cook

For Abraham. The mere hypothesis—

Allusion, only, rather,—makes the verse to run

As blank iambic, cautious of short shrift

And penance long, should Sarah know this rule

Obey'd ; yet deem (as well might be the case

Thro' feminine inconsequence) behest,

Like this, too well obey'd ; and, therefore, score

Pentameter—doubled with a measured trend

Of twice-five finger points to mark the scale—

Upon the memory of whom it should concern ;

And so, correct the matrimonial rhythm.

Lest thanks be given !—never, thus, did cark

Of jealousy find aught to feed upon

Within the borders of our tents ; nor came

There, either, from without, its mournful cry ;

As of a wolf that squats in outer gloom,

Or prowls beyond the confines of the camp,

To wail out, from the darkness mass'd around,

A dismal howl of hunger, ravening

To gnaw upon our store of happiness.

Me, only pleasing punishment befell,

" Kissing the cook :" my darling wife the cook—

None else ; for I did kiss her when the witch,

Her hands in flour, had ended all her work

Of magic, with the spell wherewith she moved

Desire thro' arch enchantment of her words

Last spoken : but lo ! for this—a loving rape

Of cherries from her lips, herself had caus'd

Did, quick, her hands, as if besieg'd within

The breadpan's walls, make sally forth in clouds

Of floury dust that blinded with defeat

Th' invader ;—or as ant-lions, shooting streams

Of sand, do blind their prey incautious of

The pitfall dug for drowning them in dust :

And as th' Aurora of the Pole bedights

The rosy northern night with whitish bars ;

So did those hands emblazon pales of flour,

With reddening accolade, upon my cheeks—·

Each turn'd to meet the blow : for well I knew

That, thro' the tender vengeance of her arms,

Did wind the love-imperill'd route to those

Dear lips—the portals whence to reave the prize,

The witch fix'd there with charms, and break

The spell she laid upon me.   My devoir,

Done gallantly, rich guerdon of her kiss

Receiv'd.——   ·

        But did the spell dissolve ?—

  Belovèd ! often have we watch'd from deck

How rising, rolling, dolphin-gambols fleck

The ocean's breast so gently musing in

The balmy air which wrought, in quiet din,

Those tinkling silver lingets thrown by sun,

Down from his treasury, to forge them on

The azure with a jewelry of light,—

And working thus did aspirate its might

Upon the twinkling waves, with zephyrs free

And breathing such a dreaminess,—that we,

Too, musèd ;—of ships ;—our voyage ;— and of that

Deep ocean bearing us upon the flat

Of its broad plain,—a gently waving lea,

Whereon sprang up, from coverts leaf'd with spray,

The tim'rous flying-fish ; as does the quail,

With startled whirring, rise to leave a trail

In air, that may the pointer's scent deceive,

And save its hunted life, or gain reprieve.

But tho' the calm mid-ocean bore our bark

That day ; yet thitherward, her course met stark,

Huge billows tumbling massy boulders on

The track, to block it with destruction : lone

Icebergs, befogg'd and floating in a drear

Of selfish pride, sent chills of aguish fear

Thro' all, to see how great the danger shunn'd

And barely 'scaped, box-haul'd the yards, when tunn'd

With over-heaviness at top, and molt,

At bottom, by the coursing undervolt

Of currents warming ocean's life, the bergs

Went toppling to their dissolution : querks

Of baffling winds did weary patience out,

Or angry, stormy gales in wrath make shout,

And threaten shipwreck ; yet the charmèd keel

Had evermore a truthful spell to feel

Wherewith, and safely find, her course thro' all:

Thro' buoys, as warders, posted on channel wall,

Thro' breezes as maidens dancing on outer green,

Thro' pampas of blue and gold in the distance seen,

Thro' offing, alone, when pilot had left our deck,

Thro' watches of night and day in the threaten'd
      wreck,

Thro' splashes of death who shotted the feet of some,

Thro' births into life, which plenish'd their vacant
      room.

   Yea: safely kept our bark her course thro' all :

All thro' the rain-gust bursting from the pall

With clouds and darkness gloom'd, and droop'd with
      weight

So drent, that scarely did a hissing jet

Of molten lightning dart a white-hot streak

To prick its bulge, before we heard the shriek

Of rents torn all across the heaven's breath,

Now awful with the thunder ; and, from the width

Of that abysm, did such a down-pour fall,

As seem'd t'would rain a deluge—but that all

The pledgèd word of God shall alway stand,

For ever good : and so, at last, in bland

And pleasant weather, did our good, staunch bark

Sail thro', from th' arch of God's bright arc

Of promise, out upon mid-ocean lying calm

And breathing dreamily ; and still thro' calm,

As thro' the storm, she kept her course as well,

Obedient to the never broken spell

Of magnet ever swaying truthfully.

Wife, companion, mine own belovéd one !—

Our married life is voyaged where the sun

Hath thrown upon its calm mid-ocean breast

The silver lingets forged (some work'd to crest

Our brows with fine drawn threads) to celebrate

Our Silver-Wedding : happiness, elate

As with the joy of dancing zephyrs, thought

No shrilling winds should blow the cold bewrought

By winter, o'er the blue and golden plain ;

Storms hung o'er us, and broke, and sent a rain

Of tears that well nigh blinded faith, in fear,

Thro' the great darkness, lest our God not near

Us was, or hid His face, in wrath not love,

From whom he chasten'd ; also, came His Dove,

A spirit of counsel and of ghostly strength,

Yet trembler with the flutterings thro' the length

Of stormy night, to bring to us the branch

All leaf'd with hope and peace, across the raunch

Of wrestling waters ; and our trust have seen

The doubtful mist made glorious with the sheen

Of brilliant polychrome, emblazoning

Archwise, to show our trust should be a thing

Enduring as th' assurance of good will

Th' All Father bears to us: our voyage, still,

Its reckoning keeps at noon, in life's calm run,

On this our Silver-Wedding Day: our Sun,

Past twelve of the clock, hath gone to turn upon

The East his lengthening shadows, but he gilds

A track with glory widening, as he builds

It westward; and th' horizon all around—

I think it touches heaven.   To the sound

As of water rippling, eddying, past her sides,

Our Life-bark holds still, on Life-ocean tides,

Its spell-bound course : I muse, as on that day

We mused in Mid-Atlantic, on the play

Of dolphins rising, rolling, diving, or

Upon the fish whose finny pinions bore

Them springing out of ocean ; and I say

In musing tone, how, like as on that day

The springing flying-fish, or dolphin's play,

Rose out of ocean, do from memory's deep

Come all these recollections,—yet the heap

Of ocean life unseen hath myriad throngs,

As greater store to memory still belongs,

Than in my lay is sung: and even now

While musing yet, our married life, I trow,

Is passing on its course, obeying spell

Wherewith a charmed magnet doth compel

The way.   And as the magnet of a ship

Controls two poles condition'd with the dip

Of single needle, by single current sway'd

Whereby th~ north and south are brethren made

Twinn'd in the line direct: so on a day—

Aye, I remember it well, as well I may,

When first those eyes, dear eyes! return'd the glance,

Magnetic with a new-born love,—a trance

Fell on my soul, and bound those spells

For ever a-renewing in the cells

Of heart to heart, in steady current blent

Thro' affection passing and repassing: lent.

And gentle, and unseen, it yet pervades

Our married lives; and oscillation vades

With wavering lessen'd into oneness, thro'

Constraint of like with unlike, in the true

Unisonance of magic undersong

Attuning souls thro' life and, all along,

Low-murmuring charm ordain'd in heaven above,

Twain to bind in one—for "God is love"

And so: the "spell could never be dissolv'd,"

Is th' answer now—from paralipse evolved
With meaning clear.

        "But will"—I hear the thought,
The woman thought, with which, this day, you sought
The mirror's false comparison with what
You think my heart may image (yet, is that
Dear self enshrined here more truthfully)—
"Will he—does he think me: ah, my hair
Was brown then, and the evening Sun would spare
Some gold dust from its stores, before the keys
Of Night should turn upon them, that the rays,
Coming aslant, might tire my tresses then
With halo of mellow light, so loved by him
That he would say I seem'd to him a form
As of the glorified: but now, these threads
Of silver weave a paler light,—yet him,
My darling, love I ever still;—but he?—
I fear me, he will not believe me now
So beautiful, on this—ah! how time flies!—
Our Silver-Wedding day."

Helen—wife!

Believe that in my heart your image stands,

With truthful likeness, full-mirror'd—

Your own dear self.   Our mortal part

Is ever dying, ever building; and

Doth ever lessen with the waste which melts

That earth-environment the inner form

Of spirit masons for a dwelling here

Not needed long.   There are who have the eyes

To see; and I am one: and so, saw thro'

Your earthly form illumin'd by the rays

Of that sun-aureole wherein you stood;

And thus beheld your spirit-form—as of

The glorified—shine thro' the earthly.   Then,

As now, and ever in the time to come—

When, in the Real Life beyond this sphere,

No longer shall we see thro' darken'd glass,

But face to face,—you were, and shall be only

Ever, imaged thus within my soul

Which closed, quickly, around your real likeness :

So, ever can I see you, only, thus—

For ever young and beautiful!

                                        My God,

I bless Thee, Lord, I bless Thy name with thanks,

On this Our Silver-Wedding Day, for this

My good, dear wife: as is most meet to thank

Thee: for a "Good Wife is of the Lord;" a gift

Of splendour, far beyond the rubies' price,

And shines, a single diamond of glory—

The Great Crown Jewel—which an husband wears

To crown his manhood.   Therefore thank I thee,

My God, for this, thy crowning earthly gift,

The only wealth which man may hope to keep,

In Heaven, of all possest by him on earth.

And hear me, Lord! now offering Thee the words

Thou gavest Israël's sweet singer to chant

With the mighty, swelling, deep-toned chords

Struck from the Great Harp:—"Lord! be Thou!

Our Shepherd; so shall we for nothing lack:

O lead Thou us; and so shall we lie down

To rest in green pastures, and slake our thirst

Beside still waters, and our souls restore,

When weary with our journeying: for Thy

Own name sake, lead Thou us, O Lord, in paths

Of Righteousness: and tho' we walk thro' that

Dark Valley of the Shadow of Death,—yea, Lord !—

No evil will we fear, if Thou be there

With us, and comfort us with aid Thy rod

And staff supply."

　　　　　Ah ! all too weak, my God,

This hand, to grasp the diapason of

Chords struck by the Chief Singer, Laureate

Of Thee for Earth : and better this, that now

I offer Thee—and simple tho' it be—

Yet better : as mine own heart's worship sung

To Thee, out of mine own heart's harp :

　　　All-Father ! who created all

　　　Thy Works, with sex to build Thy World,

　　　　　We worship Thee !

Unlike with like obey Thy call

To join, thro' sex, female with male,

And married be.

O God the Son, of Woman born,

To save Thy World a mother bare—

We honor Thine ;

Seed of the Virgin Pure ! the morn

Blush'd purity, when Thou didst bless

The Marriage Wine.

O God the Spirit ! who lighted all

Thy World to life, thro' mate to mate—

For Thou art Love ;

Thro' Thee the soul of Woman born

Is light, by Thee regenerate,—

Thou Holy Dove !

O God Triune ! who pattern'd art

In all Thy World ; so Thee, in All.

Adore we then :

Bless Thou ! the marriage trinity—

Love, Parents, Child,—until we part

No more.   Amen.

O queen !—still, all my light, my love, my life,—
This morning, sang I song of youth all rife
With love for you, my soul's whole melody :
Sweetest, best, mine own, dear, tried, true wife !—
I know you, now, my soul's whole harmony ;
And place this verse, which sings our wedded life,
At flood—its silver tide,—these gifts, among,
Of silver wrought, and by the kindly throng
Of friends, in honor brought to celebrate
Our Silver Wedding : but I know full well,
That not as least, you'll prize my song—the spell
Still binds : your lover yet ! your bald old man :
So once more listen to a heart-sung lay,—
This lay of life-long love for you,—

From Bran.

Graystead :

On this, Our Silver-Wedding Day.

V.

THE GIFTS.

THE LEGEND.

V.

TUAGOR.

I.

" Tis fitting, for Silver-Wedding meed,—
Unless this Dwarf give other rede "—
King Arthur said—" That each bestow
His goblet " (then the Dwarf bowed low)
" On this true pair whose fame shall ring
From silver harp when bard shall sing
At other Silver-Weddings, still,
In time to come.   Thy hand can thrill
The silver harp, my Taliessin !—
The silver harp thy skill did win,

In great Eisteddfod, whose awards
Named thee justly Chief of Bards,—
This thine the silver harp to thrill,
With chords, or grave, or gay, at will,
For battle, or joust with splintered lance,
Or sing sweet wounds of love's soft glance :
Chief of Bards ! none other dreading !—
Canst tune thy harp for a Silver-Wedding ? "

II.

Lest any at his skill might carp,
Taliessin took his silver harp:
The Dwarf gave look, tho' grave, not hard ;
And gravely struck one chord, the Bard,
From harp, lest distuned note should wrong.

       Taliessin's Silver-Wedding Song.

           *

" Noble knight ! and fair, true wife !
    Time a holie grace is shedding

Grace of soul, and grace of life

    Shining on your Silver-Wedding !

God made man for knightlie stour,

    Wondrous beautie gave he woman ;

Beautie, youth, love, strength, their dower,

    Wedded twain, 'gainst every foeman :

    God, twice, marriage wine gives blessing,

    Stand we here all now confessing :

Only on true man and wife,

Time a holier grace is shedding,

Grace of soul thro' wedded life,

Shining on their Silver-Wedding."

             ⸖

    The king poured wine for Taliessin,

And said :—" Thou dost as truly win

This cup that custom gives the bard,

As silver harp won by award ! "

III.

And felt they, all, that something more,
Than emptie fame, the winged years bore,
Of worth, than gain by sword or lance,
Or amorous, loose, gay dalliance;
Felt deeper care had chevalrie,
Than battle, joust, and revelrie:
True, tried faith should fill the life
Of knight and dame, true man and wife.
Pricked to heart, as sin they saw
By conscience dragged before its law,
They all resolve to mend their ways;
But doom, with mordred, and evil days
Shall come; shall come with the heartenesse;
Shall fill the land with sore distresse.

IV.

Ay me,—not long they'll feel this dread
Tho' one hath come there from the dead.

From the dead ! Yea : the Sainct Dubrece,

By wayside loue his life laid down,

Thro' vigil spent ; his soul in peace

Changed thorny chapelet for heavenlie crown :

But heaven, with the Sainct kept faith,

And sent to Arthur's hall his wraith :

In guise of Dwarf, the Sainct there stood,

And spoke the court by God his Rood.

But careless again, of name and fame,

Careless will be both knight and dame,

Thoughtless most on God or Sainct,

Faithless there in merrie Carleile,

Tho' Sainct Dubrece make sore complaint :

Thereat, the Evil one shall smile ;

The Evil one shall many beguile.

v.

But from the court and Table Round

And all the land, the evil day,

The day of doom, may now delay

A space for penitence ; for found
Therein, in life and wedlock sound,
Is noble pair, all free from blame,
Sir Cradocke and his beautious dame:
Oh, would that all may prize their fame!

VI.

The silver gifts, court-pages place
On the ladies' palfrey of gentle pace.
Quoth Sir Cradocke,—"By my sword!
A true, good wife is of the Lord,
And my best gift: so she shall ride,
This dame, my Silver-Wedding bride,
On pillion, with me, on Tuagor,—
He hath bravelie borne us both before:—
Farewell Sir Arthur, our lord and king!"
"God speed ye both, and, safe, home, bring,"—
Said King Arthur: and then did ring,
The carved rafters, as the Table Round,
With "God Speed!" made the hall resound.

VII.

Sir Cradocke, Sir Cradocke! true knight one of
three :
And chaste, one of three, is your ladie so fair :
Your fleet Tuagor* is a war-horse of three :
Tuagor, so strong and so fleet to bear
Yourself, and your ladie, safe thro' the press
And onslaught of caitiffs, or demons of air ;
Thro' spell of enchanter ; thro' wily address
And glamour of wizzard, or witch,—thro' the air
Hurtling with weapons of the powers of hell,
So strong and so fleet doth your Tuagor bear
Both you, and your ladie so fair and so chaste,
On pillion behind you, her arm round your waist.

Sir Cradocke pôst Prydain !
Of The Battle Knights Three !

---

* Tuagor, the War Horse—the spirit of counsel and ghostly
strength; which in man supports virtue (vir-virtue) and
chastitus in woman.

Rein up for a charge—

Caradoc Bran!

—Now, "God! and dear ladie!"—

Sir Cradocke, the Strong Arm'd! knightlie and well!

Your strong arm is rais'd, knightlie and well!

To guard her, and you, against powers of hell,

Or onslaught of knaves, as you crash through the
  press—

Strong-soul knight in trial and stress!

And strong is, and fleet, Tuagor! to bear

Sir Cradocke, with the Ladie so chaste and so fair!

THE SILVER WEDDING.

PART V.

THE GIFTS.

I.

THE North-west Wind, with bracing, kindly cold,

Had clear'd away the hazy evening damps

And murky halos from the tree-hung lamps:

Thro' glowing windows, hearth and houselight told

Still warmer welcome, when to Graystead roll'd

The wheels of coming friends ; and Graystead wore,

Under starlights out from heaven hung,

Bright look of cheer to those who near'd its door

As wedding guests : the friends with gifts and token

To crown the Silver-Wedding of twain who clung

Thro' life, God-join'd with tie that naught had broken.

II.

With common purpose, as for greater state,
The wedding guests a train had form'd, before
The highway led their course to Graystead gate,
Where thro' now, carriage after carriage bore
A friendly load to land at Graystead's door.
And greetings after greetings kindly pass'd
Exchange of friendship, thro' long years, amass'd
Against the years of dearth and loss, when corn
And oil fail; and only stand, forlorn
Tho' flourishing, the almond tree and thorn.
Nor only friends of youth their greeting made;
But youth itself was there, and reverence paid;
For Bran and Helen's house was one where youth
Met Pleasure kindly led by faithful Truth.

III.

Then,—as gather'd there in Graystead hall,
The greetings past, they stood in silence, all,

Save that the huge, hall chimney roar'd aloud
Its welcome still,—one, from the wedding guests
Beforehand chosen spokesman for the rest,
One bright of eye tho' age his shoulders bow'd,
Stepp'd forth and thus the worthy pair addrest:

IV.

" True-married ! we come to you, to celebrate
Your Silver-Wedding: and, with forethought sown
And ripen'd to fruit in counsel, are we come
To you: as having judged you worthy twain
Whose Silver-Wedding claims far other meed
Of honour and observance than is dealt
Mere, passing, blaring anniversaries,
Quack advertisements on wayside milestones
Of Time. For, taking counsel among ourselves,
Who most of us have known you long and well:
And knowing well how truly man and wife
Ye twain together bound as one have lived
After God's own holy ordinance,

Wherein is symbol blent with blessing

For all create of God and, by His will,

Continuing creation, each the like

With like-unlike, all after their own kind ;

Believing, too, that thus the model set

In union of God-join'd and life-true pair,

And thus the symbol and significance :

We, after counsel, found us all agreed,

Held that a Silver-Wedding mark'd a point

Where culminates the upheav'd range of life,

Whereon is beacon set that all should heed,

Should tend with a common zeal, to keep alive

The signal shining for the common weal.

And thinking thus, with one accord was made

Decision that our tribute to your worth,

At this your Silver-Wedding, should denote,

Not only honour, and the love of friends,

But mark a sense of common welfare bound

With loyal married life : no vulgar show,

As if each guest thus sought to advertise

In troy of jeweller's hardware all his wealth,

Should any make ; but all should give the gift

Of all, betokening the love of all,

And wrought to show a meaning symbolized

For all, those giving, as for those endow'd.

But furthermore, that each of us might show

An individual regard, it was held,

An added lesser gift of modest cost

Should show how each would do you reverence.

  " And much we cast about "—continued he

The spokesman, making reverence as he spoke—

" How art should fashion best our gifts in silver,

To show the meaning, thus, our hearts would speak ;

Till one among us, one much read in lore

And legend of an ancient time, then told

A tale of Arthur's court : how thither, once,

There came an unknown dwarf, who honour brought

On married pair of noble knight and dame,

Thro' magic gifts,—a mantle, gold-wrought horn,

And knife wherewith to carve the boar's head, true :

P

And how that Arthur hearing that the day,

Whereon this noble pair had won these gifts,

Scor'd five and twenty faithful married years

For them, ordain'd, in honour of their worth,

The use and custom of the Silver-Wedding;

And how, for further honour, king and court

Each gave to them the silver cup wherein

With wine he pledged that noble knight and dame

Long life and all prosperity.   This tale

Soon made us all of one consenting mind

What gifts to choose as best betokening

The honour all would show your Silver-Wedding —

The more "—here humour mingled with his speech—

"That since a Cambrian pedigree ascends

To Adam, and in law is absolute

As title deed;* we hold you, from your name,

As from your own and your dear lady's worth,

One who may most justly claim descent

---

* Fosbrooke's Antiquities.

From that Sir Cradocke the doughty knight, with
    dame

So fair and true, of whom the legend tells.

And therefore we—but let the gifts themselves

Set forth the meaning and the love of friends

Expressed in tribute to your sterling worth,

To crown, O time-tried pair, your Silver-Wedding!"

    At sign from him, there enter'd then the hall

A smiling, youthful train; young men and maidens

Bringing in, on massive silver salver

Borne, the costly Silver-Wedding token.

For it was wrought with cost, since all—and some

Were wealthy—had given as were their means

To show their love: and so the gift of all

Was worthy of all, but advertised the wealth

Of none; yet signified the love of all.

    The base that rested on the silver salver

Was silver thickly armor'd all with gold,

And toward the centre rose as swells a knoll

Uplifted from a plain: and on this height,

On legs carv'd all of gold as lion paws,

Was held a drinking horn; a bison's horn,

Short-curv'd and broad, and polish'd ebon-black,

Gold-wrought with bands of vine and leaves of grapes,

From tip to brim: and also, round the brim

Was bound an antique crown of gold, and gold

The inside lined; and, after ancient fashion,

Gold drinking pegs, that pierced the lining, mark'd

The measure of the wine: and on the base,

Beneath the horn, between the carv'd gold paws,

A goodly silver platter sate, whereon

Was cunningly, in silver likewise, wrought

A boar's head and a knife, a silver harp,

The symbol of will, with will, in concord blent,

Beside the platter with boar's head, gave

The horn support in front; and over the horn,

With draping folds spread gracefully, was thrown

A mantle wrought of silver enamell'd all

A royal purple; save where a narrow stripe,

Edging the purple gold with soften'd glow

A mellow border form'd, on lustrous brink
Of silver lining all the purple cloud ;
And one great pearl, an orient pearl of price,
Was set in gold to form the mantle's clasp.

And as the youthful band bore in this gift,
It seem'd as though to Bran and Helen came
A train of honor following their married life
Even upwards from their youth, to crown
Their Silver-Wedding.

                    Then each wedding guest
Placed on the silver salver, his silver cup
Modest, but solid: and each cup was mark'd
To whom the gift, and with the giver's name
Engraved with motto: " Honour the Silver-Wedding. '
And the goblets heap'd and weighted so the salver,
That glad were they who bore the load
To place it on a buffet standing near.

  " Kind dear friends"—began then Bran to speak:
But all the fullness of his heart well'd up and drown'd
His speech: so that he paused: and simply thank'd

Their guests for all the honour done them both —

"But" said he—"most honour be to her,

The faithful wife and mother; wherefore, pray,

Let these your gifts so rich and rare, be given

As it were to her: that thus, thro' her, may come

To me, a share of this great honour done

By you, dear friends, our Silver-Wedding."

  "O ay," said he, the same who spoke before

For all; as though he sought in sympathy

To hide with humour Bran's emotion—"ay,

Thrice ay, t'were well—it is a drinking horn—

To make the gift thro' her, since may—who knows?—

Our fair hostess, your dear lady, claim

Prayerful dominion over drinking horn

And cups. There be now strange things heard in air,

And strange things done and seen—so haste my friend,

Lest a sudden, a bacchanal rage of prayer

Sieze all these fair dames present here, before—

Haste! my friend, fill drinking horn and cup—

We pledge in wine 'God speed the Silver-Wedding!'"

Thro' that resilience with which emotion

Springs unbent, laugh'd Helen and the ladies

And Helen gracefully accepting then

The token, said she took the gift as made,

But fear'd no ill therefrom ; since she could see

How plain the drinking pegs, in gold-text, mark'd

The sentence : " *Using as not abusing.*"

                                  Wine

Was brought; and one, a priest, now bent with weight

Of years and reverend calling,—who had joined

The hands of Bran and Helen in their youth,

Blessing in the Master's name their marriage wine—

Then, seeing that these twain had lived together

After God's own holy ordinance

As one, rais'd hands and, now the second time,

Bless'd wine for them, at this their Silver-Wedding.

Then from the gold-wrought horn refill'd at need,

The guests their goblets fill'd, and all there drank—

" God speed the Silver-Wedding—that so may these,

Our honour'd friends, their wedded life find moor'd

At anchor safe again, near where the sun
Unclouded on their Golden-Wedding day
Shall go to gild, against there coming, th' isles
Of the Blessèd, and mountain peaks, and all
The sleeping land rising to meet the day ! "

   Bran and Helen, from the gold-wrought horn,
Then pledged their guests, with meet acknowledge-
    ment.

And scarce had finish'd : when a servitor—
An ancient white-hair'd servitor whose boast
Was how his master's boyhood days had vex'd
His charge with prankish mischief—interrupted
The bee-like hum of converse which declar'd
A ceremony over, with his prompt made
Announcement of the wedding supper serv'd,
At which, laughingly, the youthful band, again,
Took up the salver ; and, follow'd by the rest,
March'd to place the gifts upon the board.

   What need to say that Meadows kept her word?—
That naught of roast, or boil or bake, or crust,

Did fail of savoury witness to high art,

And science, at this Silver-Wedding feast ;

Or why detail the course and incidents

Of feast and joy-making ? much the same,

Chief differing in degree, or means, or state,

All feasts have been since, now these thousand years

And more, the people sat down to meat, and rose

To play ; and this grave epithalamium

Chants rather a chorale of the Silver-Wedding,

Singing its symbolism for the theme,

Than moves to blitheful measures Hymen leads

In youth.   Yet was the dance not wanting there ;

For Bran and Helen, with all the elder folk,

Sacrifice to youth in an ancient dance.

And games were play'd ; and kindly pleasure ruled

With chasten'd joy their Silver-Wedding evening ;

And songs were sung—nay even he, the bent

Old man, the marshal of the gifts, was moved

To sing ; and shrewdly smiling, first he told

The younger folk his song was well to learn

For love, and love-making, as for all things else ;
And then, thus quaver'd he :—

THE SONG OF TIME.

As wrong is he who knows not how to wait,
    As he who ever is too late :
Know this of *ohne hast*, of *ohne rast* *—
Go sometimes slowly, a little sometimes fast,
    On safest course, the middle way,
    That sun-path rounding all our day.

" Perhaps," said he, when he had sung, " my song
May hint our day well spent more ways than one :
And that, with all the times for other things,
There also is a time to sleep : a time
For all—old-folk and young—to be in bed."
To which, good-humour'dly, assented all
Agreed that Time had right to speak a hint
In plain language : and leave-taking commenc'd,

---

* Goethe.—" Without haste, without rest."

And many the kind hopes, and kind wishes, spoken :

And at the last, with one acclaim, all, guests

And host, join'd in "God speed the Silver-Wedding!"

 Bran stood watching his departing guests

Until a star-lit grove beyond his grounds

Had hid the last : and as is oft the wont

Of one, to look to learn what of the night,

Before he turn from parting guests to go

Within ; so Bran look'd up, and saw, with heart

All grateful, how the silver star-lamps spread

A calm, clear, steady light throughout the heavens,

On this his Silver-Wedding night.   Howbeit,

Whether from reaction ; or that, all

True human happiness must rest on chastening ;

Bran Cradocke, looking up to heaven, said

In low, sad tone,—"*per aspera ad astra.*"

But, none less grateful, he : and gratitude

Was his, that sought to render thanks, thro' those

In need, back to the Giver : so would he now

Shelter even the wayside tramp he saw

Beneath a huge oak, standing near the gates
To watch the passing guests.   And Bran, going
Toward him,—"God of mercy, and Good Shepherd!—
Helen!—mother!—our son!—the lost is found!"
For he knew him from afar; and ran,
And fell upon his neck, and kissed him:
And took the wan, starv'd form beneath the oak
Whose mighty limb reach'd thro' the star-lit night,
As tho' an arm stretch'd out from heaven to give
The lost one back; and in his own arms bore
He him, houseward, to meet the trembling mother
Hastening toward them: and between them held,
Bran and Helen hailed their new-found son
Home, to warm and feed him at their hearth.

   Ah, sacred joy of that house: and none
But words that tell of kindred angel-joy
Over the one sinner that repenteth, may
Have power to speak it.

               Came then all unbid
The household: but dismiss'd were soon, by beck

Authoritative, of their white-hair'd chief,

The ancient servant: but himself would stay

A space, by virtue of his service length,

To brisk the fire before he left the hall.

And Meadows, too, made brief stay, bringing food;

But soon would go to make, she said, a posset,

And—said the mother—a fire in the nursery,

And there, to-night, his bed. Then, left alone

(For long asleep were now the younger children)

With their long-lost son, the parents warm'd

And cherish'd him; for he was sick, and wasted,

And had been long absent from their hearth.

And his father forgave him all, and bless'd him

Now humble as little child: and then, when they

Had succour'd him, the mother would have him,

Between them holpen, to the nursery;

For she said he was as born again

To her, and he,—" Yea, mother, for I had come

To die near you, somewhere, unworthy to come

To you; and the life twice-given from you both,

God helping me, shall be, indeed, new life."

There spoke the strong soul of the father in him—

Strong in humility wherewith God lifts

The wrestler up from all the overthrow

And wretchedness of sin.   And too, the frame

Of the wanderer, stalwart copy of his father's,

Emaciate though it was, gave hope that still

Might brawny strength return to him again,

Thro' patience of recoverance.   But now,

All weak was he, as a sick child; and as

A sick child, would the mother have him near;

To watch, and tend, and sooth to rest.   Nor might

He tell, until returning strength repaid

Long days and nights of anxious watching,

How wilfulness, chafing at wise governance,

Rejected it, and wrought a soul-weakness

That fell before the passions rushing in

With riotous living that wasted him; until

The son of their prayers had prostrate lain among

The potsherds, feeding on the husks of vice.

And losing his faith, the world became to him

Without a God ; and so, his evil way of life

Countenanc'd suspicion of crime ; and he

Tho' innocent, and afterwards prov'd innocent,

Was driven out from men, to misery

And want—yet had, he said, of his father's strength

Enough, rather to beg, or starve, than steal.

But never could he close all his soul against

His mother's voice, hearing it in the night :

As tho' a child held in her arms, he heard

Her singing songs of one who was Good Shepherd

That brought home in his arms lost sheep, coming

Over hills all mellow-bright with golden sunset—

Whereon, the soul of the mother hearing this

Sang, inwardly, the Song of the Virgin Mother,

For this Salvation sent thro' her.   Also,

He told how he, repentant, would have come

Home to them, but was ashamed : and yet

Must come, constrain'd beyond him, to their gates

To look on, from afar, the honour crowning
The lives to which he was but grievous cross
And cruel thorn. " And there," said he, with holy,
Filial tears, " my father found and took
Me, perishing with want and misery,
To his great heart; and blesséd mother, you—
You sav'd your son."

           This told when strength return'd :
But now, seeing his weakness, Helen sat
As in his childhood, by his bed, with arm
Beneath his pillow, softly placed : and gently,
All the mother soothed her child to rest.

Sweet is the rest

Of the Soul come home to God,

Humble as little child :

Sweet, as on breast

Of a mother, sleep of child

Soothed from the pain of the chastening rod,

Soothed by the lullaby, low and mild,

Vibrating softly the mother's breast

Thrilling and singing the child to rest :

Sweet is this rest.

THE EPILOGUE.

THE EPILOGUE.

I.

METAPHYSICS, and discourse on God,
In larder as from library heard! *Where else!*—
And wherefrom better, than from whence began
All movement of man's mind and thought on God.
For God's first altar was the primal hearth,
Where simple, uncult man, in thankful hope,
Denying to himself a part of food,
His toil'd for food, made daily sacrifice
Of offerings burnt, and of libation pour'd,
In loss to gain ; that so, Propitiation
Might follow on Renunciation ; on

Thanksgiving, favour, from the Power unseen,

Let in, around, above him felt.   And then,

His mind on thought fed,—"Where, and what, is
      He?

And all things, what are they? and what are we?

How get more food? how keep and dress this Earth?

I think—therefore I am: but wherefore birth?

And death? and grief wherefore, and wherefore
      mirth?

II.

    For thinking man lives not by bread alone:

His soul to die refuses, seeking food

Immortal; searching thro' religion, art,

And science; even thro' his energies

Of building and destroying; blinded oft,

Thro' very eagerness of search, by dust

He stirs from cracks and crannies nearest him,

And for a while his sight be dimmed: but tears

Of baffled immortality to brim

Of strain'd eyes rise, and wash away his fears,

His doubting error, and material hindrance,--

Clearing his spirit eye, for search of food:

And the sound, sane aggregate of human soul

And mind, self-conscious that, tho' race and species,

Earth adapted, die, yet shall the soul

Individual, loosed from chemic thrall,

Take up a body incorruptible

Raised from incorruption,—aye, the sane, whole
    mind,

The mankind-soul, *knows* man to surely live

On to immortality; by bread

Not only, even in the flesh; but live

Here, and hereafter, by every word of God.

But nations wending thro' the drear Sahara

Of materialism may, like caravans

Not timely kneeling, there be overwhelm'd

With sure destruction, and behold no more

The calm, blue heaven and the golden sun

Enduring still in glory, beyond, above
The storm of pitiless, cutting, material fact,
Which, blinding first, shall bury them alive.

III.

   Where better, then, than under roof
Of home, which nursery, larder, library covers,
Be centr'd all of God and man's behoof,
In union true of God-join'd, life-long lovers.
For nations are by man and woman built,
And nations fall thro' man and woman's guilt.
Without God in the family! this it means—
Without God in the World! nay worse, it means
The World without a God.   Never ignor'd
Be God; but under family roof-tree be ador'd
As Teraphim, The Three in One, the God Triune,
Who blends the All in one harmonious tune
The God All Father who creates the All
The All to build thro' law in loving thrall
And quest of mate to mate, thro' male-female

The God who heard free will's despairing wail

For help from choosing wrong from right; and
    hearing,

So lov'd the world, that with His highest work

His Holy Spirit wed: the God, who nearing

Humanity for finishing His work.

The world so lov'd of Him, gave Christ, His Son

Made man, to death; that victory might be won

By man from death. This God, with power divine,

At Cana made and bless'd the marriage wine.

IV.

Well may a Silver-Wedding crown the state

And being of the All of God create,

Since All builds All thro' sex, thro' male-female,

From lowest up to highest, thro' the the scale

That ends in man. And in the God-join'd pair

Of God's best work, who God's own image bear,

Are type and blessing there all culminate,

Of all God's work thro' quest of mate to mate,

Where, in a Silver-Wedding, culminate

Is cycle of a generation.   Thine,

O God! therefore, the miracle divine,

At Cana wrought to bless The Marriage Wine.

   Then awoke I from my dream.   For I had dream'

And in my dream it was as tho' one stood

Singing on the porch a morning song

In the bright, glad beams of a rising sun,

Rejoicing in the fresh, spring morning air.

And it was one from whom my being came ;

Who, from a life of pain relcas'd, had chang'd

The priest's white robe he wore on earth, for robes

Brighter, of those become the kings and priests

To God : and as he sang I knew his voice ;

But scarcely could behold him thro' the crevice

That strain'd a slender ray faint shimmering thro'

Clos'd window blinds of a room all darken'd else.

For so it seem'd, that I was in a room

Not open'd yet to day ; and, in the dark,

Sat, at an organ triple-bank'd with keys ;

Whereon groping for keys and stops, I sought

To interpret the song of him who, bright of face,

Stood singing in the sunlight. And with him

I sought to join in song. But thro' the haste

Lest I should lose his song, my hands trembled,

Groping in the dark ; and many chords

I miss'd ; and so could only sing in part—

Nay only in part heard I, thro' those thick walls :

And the organ was as a great organ, swell'd

To sound by fanning wings unseen ; so great

Its volum'd power, I could not master it,

Groping in the dark ; and so, in part

Only, could I join the song of him

Who in the sunlight sang : yet tho' in part

Only, I knew I sang the truce of God ;

For symbol, weaving in an old-world tale.

L'ENVOY.

Give most honour to faithful wife and mother :
She hath right to it more than any other,
Who thro' wedded life, virgin soul retaining,
Who on marriage dishonour never bringing,
Trains up children, with gentle hand restraining,
Trains towards heaven her children round 1
    clinging,
Rules her husband, him good man never knowing,
(Tho' known well, in the gates with elders sitting :
There all matters weigh'd—mostly logic splitting,)
On all, house and home, comfort dear bestowing ;
And fair children all, virgin maid of honour,
Lives unwedded in duty laid upon her,
Shall have worship, because of th' angels seeing ;
Life-true woman is God's best, purest being.
Place aux dames ici ! dames du moyen âge ! oui,

L'ENVOY.

Place d'honneur! let each heart be crying,

View tried woman true,—maiden aunt, or

But most honour to faithful wife and moth

She hath right to it more than any other:

Tried, true, dearest wife, Dwarf's eye never

Lo! true Queen is she! crown'd at Silve